The
Straight Man
by Kent Nelson

A Black Lizard Book
from
Creative Arts Book Company

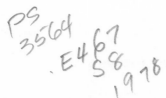

This project is supported in part by a grant
from the National Endowment for the Arts in
Washington, D.C., a Federal agency.

Black Lizard Books are published by Creative
Arts Book Company, 833 Bancroft Way,
Berkeley, CA 94710.

Library of Congress Catalog Card #77-88656
ISBN 0-916870-11-1

Cover Design by Michael Patrick Cronan

To the Family

1/   The bar had once been mentioned in *Time* magaine as an infamous hangout for dope people on Florida's west coast. The bitter-faced man sat at a red and white gingham covered table idly sipping a draught beer and watching the loser chicks wriggle to the blaring juke box. He'd been seen around, yet was known by virtually no one. He looked too straight. Those that knew anything about him considered him a strange, doper middleman. They were partially right. He didn't want to steal anymore. He didn't want to carry a gun. He just wanted to make money the easy way, by dealing. There was the usual fear of a bust, but narcs and finks usually ended up in Great Tampa Bay, so few of the dealers worried much.

His contact walked up, and sat down. "Hey, man. How ya been? Here I am, right on time. Lemme get something cold."

He rose and walked to the bar. He wore a cowboy hat, kept a scrapbook of his Viet Nam experiences and worked in the straight world as a mechanic. He was a sometime lid dealer. The cowboy hat was well known and exchanged words with at least half a dozen freaks on his way back to the table. He sat down, nodded, said, "I hear there's some Colombo in town?"

The straight man said, "That's right, man. All good bud. I can turn to you for two an L.B., singles, or one eighty-five quantity. How many you want?"

"Well, I gotta try it man, you know?"

"No problem. Just tell me how many. I'll bring it over, and you can smoke right out of the pound."

"Can we do a thing tonight?"

"Yeah, if my man's home."

"Okay, I'll take one right now. You know where I live, right?"

"Same place? That trailer?"

"Yeah. Same place."

"Right. I'll be there in two hours. That'll be ten o'clock."

"All right, brother. We're wired. We got a deal."

They shook hands by grabbing each other's thumbs. No one seemed to know why that method of shaking hands had become the way. The straight man rose and left. He got into his compact and drove six blocks to a freak area of low rent cottages. It looked like someone was home at the cottage he had in mind. He parked, walked to the door and knocked. An attractive brunette opened the door, smiled, and let him in.

Her old man, stoned as usual, said, "Hey bro, what's happening? Sit down and get high."

The straight man sat on the floor with him. "Listen, what will you turn a single of Colombo to me for?"

He took a hit of the proferred number and passed it back. The woman was cutting oranges in the kitchen.

The dealer took a deep drag and said, "Oh, man, I can't turn singles for less than 175, even to you. You know that."

"That's good enough. I'm supposed to turn one tonight at ten. I want you to front me. If he likes it, we might be able to do quantity. Say, this shit sure is good. I'm getting a buzz already."

The dealer looked at the straight man and said, "Look, this shit is a front to me. I got to turn it, or give it back. When can I have the money by?"

"You'll have it by eleven. I give you my word. I haven't fucked up yet, have I?"

"Okay, man, okay."

The dealer rose and went into his bedroom. Momentarily he returned with a three foot cardboard box and a green plastic garbage bag that appeared full. From the cardboard box he removed a triple beam scale with a large pan and set it up on the floor. From the garbage bag he removed handfuls of marijuana, buds and stems, and filled the pan. The scale registered fourteen ounces. From the bottom of the garbage bag he wighdrew a couple of handfuls of "shake," a mixture of leaf and seed. Moments later, there was roughly seventeen ounces in the pan. The woman brought in two large glasses of orange juice.

The dealer said, "Hey mama, thanks. Bring a paper bag, will ya?"

She went back to the kitchen and returned with a brown supermarket bag. The pound was placed inside it. The scale was carefully put away. From the shake of the garbage bag more leaf was placed in some Blanco y Negro papers, and they smoked.

After a few pulls, the dealer studied the joint and said, "Look at that collar. That's how you tell if the reefer is any good. Shows you how much of that good tic resin is in it."

The woman giggled.

The straight man grinned, "I'm hip man. I can't stop smiling."

They all started laughing.

After a while the straight man said, "Well, I got to get out on the street and make a sale. See you later."

He rose and went out to his car. The cool night air cleared his head. He looked up and saw the stars, clean and distant, out of reach. He thought of his ex-wife, long gone now, and cursed his stupidity. He occasionally wrote her a letter, but she was a Scorpio and they traditionally never forgive an affront to their egos.

Letting his mind drift, he drove for thirty minutes to an obscure trailer park out in the piney woods. The cowboy hat was home. He parked, carried the shopping bag to the trailer, and knocked. Cowboy hat, still wearing the hat, stuck his head out. The straight man wondered if he ever took it off. He'd never seen him without the damn thing.

The hat said, "Hey, man. Come on in. Want a beer?"

"Yeah, okay. I hope you got some papers. This is the best shit I've seen since '69."

It was a good sized trailer with a large living room and the kitchen looking down into it. The straight man sat on the couch and placed the bag on the small, hand-carved coffee table. The stereo, in the corner, had a Pink Floyd album on it. Cowboy hat sat down with a couple of cans of Budweiser. They popped their tops, cowboy rolled a number, cranked it up, took two deep drags and passed it with the comment, "Tastes good."

The straight man took a small drag and returned it. Two drags later the cowboy rose, went up to his kitchen, opened a drawer and came back with two hundred dollars in tens, twenties and fives.

After a rapid count, the straight man pushed the roll into his pocket. "Hat," he said, "I'm only making a nickel on this shit. If you want some more, just call me. You got my number. Just say how many six-packs you need and what time to be here, okay?"

The cowboy hat, giggling and chuckling, said, "Okay, man. I got some people coming from Atlanta. Maybe we can do something."

"Okay, good buddy. Later."

The straight man left. He drove until he saw a convenience store, pulled up in front, withdrew the roll, peeled off twenty-five for himself and placed it in a different pocket. A little later he knocked at the cottage door.

2/ At one a.m. the straight man parked at a restaurant near the University. He walked into the dimly lit bar area and saw the man he hoped to find. The cat was a bit of an idiot, but he was on top of a steady Jamaican connection. The idiot had stringy blond hair, had once been a social worker and now wanted only money. He talked, dreamt, and worshipped money. He drank only Heinekens beer.

The straight man sat next to him at the bar. "Hey, idiot, how ya been?"

"Fine, just fine. I've got a thousand pounds of dynamite red-bud. Best I've ever had. I can turn to you for one thirty-five, quantity. It won't be here long."

The man said nothing, merely nodded. The idiot talked too much.

He thought about the last time he'd been here with his ex-wife. She'd been dressed up and had looked beautiful. He'd made some enemies that night by telling some fat slobs not to cuss in front of her. He drank a Budweiser, and silently wished she would answer one of his letters.

Finally he turned to the idiot and said, "Okay, man. I'll see what I can do. Later."

He drove to his apartment slowly, thinking about her. She'd never said the words, not once, and he believed he still loved her.

3/   The next day was bright and sunny but not the usual power-sapping heat. The telephone rang about eleven and the straight man answered. A strange voice said, "Hey, we're friends of Moe's. He said if we got down here to look you up."

"Oh, yeah. What do you do?"

"I'm a mechanic, just like Moe."

"Fine. Why don't you drop by." The straight man gave them directions. He'd known Moe for over fifteen years. Moe was a pound dealer in Chicago. The regular people had been busted at O'Hare airport because the names on the tickets and the I.D. hadn't matched. The cops had examined the luggage and found thirty thousand that hadn't been declared. The I.R.S. had the money now and probably wouldn't ever give it back.

The straight man called Moe long distance. "Hey, shithead, how ya been? I just got a call from some people. Did you put anyone on to me? How's your old lady?"

"Oh, yeah. They're okay. Jay and Ted. Jay is short, has black hair, and his partner is tall, shoulder-length blond hair, and wears glasses. I've done some things with them. My old lady is giving me a pain, but I got a girlfriend, so I'm gettin' by."

"Okay, man. Talk to ya later." They hung up.

The straight man and Moe had worked together before. They went back to the days when they'd been leather-jacketed punks on the street. Moe had done a stretch in reform school once. He'd gone by to see his girlfriend and she'd answered the door with the words, "Go away, I don't love you anymore," and closed the door. He'd rung the bell again and gotten the same words. After the third time he realized she was serious. He wandered to a parking lot and stole a Corvette. While driving it around, he gave a ride to one of the gang standing on a corner. The police began chasing them. Moe ran past seven roadblocks before he ran out of gas. That evening had netted him six months, plus costs, and the reputation as an excellent wheel man.

Years later it had been alcohol that had gotten him a second bust. He and another friend had been down in Chatanooga. They'd been drinking the local moonshine for hours and become insane.

Moe drove through the plate glass window of a Cadillac agency showroom and minutes later drove out another window in a brand new Cadillac. They played rat race with the police until Moe underjudged a turn and crashed inside a laundry. Moments later, when the police stormed in, Moe and his friend were standing there, laughing like crazy, throwing laundry at each other. He was given a choice: prison or the Army.

When he came back from the Army he was a quieter cat, more interested in dealing dope than stealing. The same applied to the straight man. Dealing drugs didn't pay as well, but the risk wasn't as great, and in jails, next to the international jewel thieves, drug people had the highest status.

4/ There was a knock at the door. It was a retired dope dealer and his wife. They lived in some small town out in the woods of north Florida. They were happy and healthy and they had both known the straight man's ex-wife. He was glad to see them. They stayed for a while, shared a number and left to visit other people while they were in town.

As the straight man watched them pull away, a snow white Lincoln Continental pulled up. The driver was short, slight, and had black hair and a moustache. The other was six foot, had shoulder length blond hair, wore glasses, and appeared to be in excellent shape. They walked up, and all shook hands. They said their names were Jay and Ted. They came inside. The man felt something wrong, but Moe had said they were okay. They all smoked a number and got to the point. Jay did the talking.

"We're here to cop. We need about five hundred pounds. We've got other people with our mobile home. Can you do us any good?"

The straight man nodded, said, "I'll see," and called the idiot. The idiot wasn't home, but his ex-junkie girlfriend was. He left a message for the idiot to come over by seven that night. He went back to Jay and Ted and told them that they ought to come back about eight. They'd all go to dinner. They left.

At five the idiot knocked on the door. "Hey, man. C'mon in. Want a beer?"

"Yeah. Got any Heinekens?"

"Fuck you, aristocrat. I got Old Milwaukee, take it or leave it."

"Okay, okay. Gimme one of them."

11

They sat on the straight man's couch. When he'd been married his ex-wife had done the rolling. He thought about her. He rolled a number. He decided to tell the idiot what he'd been called for.

"Listen up. There's a couple people in town from Chicago. They want to cop five hundred pounds. Are you on top of that much? It's more than I've ever handled. I'll put them on to you. All I want is a nickel. Sound fair?"

"Yeah, sure. Did you see the money?"

"Nope, but my man in Chicago says they're okay. They'll be back at eight. We can all go to dinner."

The idiot nodded, getting the in-the-know look on his face. He smiled. "Okay. But you let me take care of everything."

"Fine. I just want a nickel, that's all. You can make as much as you want."

The dealer rose, "I'll be back at eight. Just let me take care of everything." He left.

The straight man considered the possibilities. With an estimated twenty-five hundred dollars from this deal he could go away, maybe even round up his ex-wife. Maybe they could start again, somewhere else. Maybe Oregon. He'd get a job, go super-straight. They'd be happy. Have kids. He sat on his couch and smoked the dope.

The phone rang. It was the ex-wife of an acquaintance. She wanted to get laid. He said he'd be along about eleven and hung up. He left his apartment and walked down the street to another dealer's place. This other dealer only turned cocaine. He was home. A gram of coke that had only been stepped on once or twice was forty dollars. The straight man bought one for his date that night.

5/   At eight, Jay and Ted were back. They came in and sat down. The straight man rolled a number. As he rolled, he mentioned that he'd been married once.

"Shit!" said Jay. "You get what you pay for. Forget getting serious about any chick. Forget her. Be like me. I'm into V.Y.G. myself."

"What's V.Y.G.?"

"Very Young Girls," he grinned.

Ted remained impassive. The vibes from these two were still wrong. There was a knock at the door. It was the idiot. Introductions were made. They all walked outside. It was decided that the roomiest car was the Continental. Jay drove and Ted rode shotgun; the idiot and the straight man shared the back.

They took the Interstate north for a way and turned off at a steakhouse the straight man liked. He'd taken his ex-wife there many times. They'd even had their own "special" table.

He made sure that they sat at a different one. They ordered drinks. Jay was insulted when he didn't get exactly what he'd ordered, and let the waitress know. He was unnecessarily cruel. The meal was good. Jay did the talking. He told a story about some Jamaicans he knew in Miami who'd shot each other up, and about how one who'd been shot with a .45 had been up and around the next day. When the meal was over they left and returned to the straight man's apartment.

The idiot took Jay and Ted to meet some of his people. The man watched them go, hoping things would be all right. He turned on the television and rolled himself a number.

6/   At eleven the straight man knocked on his date's door. A short Italian girl opened it with a smile. She was wearing hot pants and a T-shirt. The stereo was playing some Dutch sax. He sat on the couch while she went to make drinks. By the time she came back he'd pulled out the gram of coke and dumped it on the coffee table. She went back to the kitchen for a knife. They talked idly about mutual friends and acquaintances as he cut the lines. He rolled a dollar bill and did a line. She eagerly did a line. They looked at each other and smiled. Five minutes later the coke was all snorted and she lit a number of her own stash. They sat close, and talked, and fondled each other. After a while she led him to her king size bed. They made slow love. He pretended she was his ex-wife. She didn't pretend. He left at two. When he got home, Jay and Ted were waiting.

Jay was angry. "What shit, man. I was blind-folded. Driven in circles. Taken to some barn, and there was five hundred pounds of wet shit. Grown locally, or something. You people here are a bunch of fuck-ups."

"Slow down. Tell me what happened real slow. Sit down. Relax. Want a beer? You both were blindfolded?"

"No. Just me. Ted stayed with that idiot. I went riding around with some friend of his named Brad. He's a drifty dude, too. The reefer was shit! I'm ready to go to Miami right now. Fuck this. Fuck all this." He accepted a beer, so did silent Ted. The straight man rolled a number. There was a knock at the door. It was the idiot.

"Listen," he said, "Brad is sorry. We just wanted to give you a better price than our other people. That's all. Tomorrow I'll take you to meet some other people. I'll get you prime Jamaican red-bud, but it's gonna cost you. I mean, like, can you handle a buck-and-a-half a pound for five hundred? That's about as good as we can do."

Jay looked at Ted, who nodded "yes." The straight man lit the number, took a drag, and passed it on. He was tired. Tired of the dope world. Tired of balling chicks he didn't care about. Tired of the whole Tampa scene.

7/ The straight man had been in Tampa seven years. When he'd gone to visit his mother for Christmas nine years before, he'd been drafted. Two years later he was more interested in drugs than in armed robbery. When he'd been discharged, the main drug import points had been Miami for cocaine, Savannah for heroin, and Florida's west coast for marijuana. The hard drug situation was closed but the weed scene had been open to all.

Tampa, whose sister city was Baranquilla, Colombia, was a town experiencing a boom. It had been a sleepy little port until the Spanish-American War of 1898, when Teddy Roosevelt and his Rough Riders had come to town. Then again, it became sleepy.

The twenties boom hadn't changed it much. As little as ten years previously a bored policeman had been arrested for shooting out streetlights. It had been the last city in the United States to build its streets out of brick. Now it had become an overgrown small town with people flowing in daily. Whatever cohesiveness it once had was disappearing. It was becoming another megalopolis similar to Miami or Los Angeles. The dozen families that had once kept it quiet were losing their hold. There wasn't much to do except drink and fuck. It had its annual invasion by pirates, a poor imitation of New Orleans' Mardi Gras, when the Rotary Club could dress up and get drunk. What nightclubs there were catered to visiting firemen who wanted something strange. Chain motels with a bar did a good business.

There was also big money to be made. Construction and real estate speculation had built several banks. While Las Vegas had its little old ladies spending their Social Security checks on the slot machines, Tampa, and its neighbor across the Bay, St. Petersburg, had its ladies at the dog tracks, while the more affluent could to to the horse tracks, or even Jai Alai. There were few bookies. Underground gambling, bolita, and the cock fights that took place every Sunday, were controlled by the old families.

Fortunes in marijuana had also been made. There was the story of one entrepreneur who had purchased a yacht. It had a large mortgage on it. He'd had good contacts and told various dealers on the U.S. east coast a location. He said he'd be there one of three nights, giving them the dates. There was a gathering of people at a deserted point on the Florida west coast. The ship didn't show the first night, nor the second. None of the people were hostile with each other. They sat around talking and roasting marshmallows. On the third night, just at dusk, the yacht slipped in. The biggest dealer, from New York, had gone aboard first. He'd bought enough to fill his truck. The truck had gotten stuck in the sand. The other dealers had pushed the truck through the sand to the road, and he'd been on his way. The yacht owner paid for his ship and made a quarter of a million to boot that night.

Even so, with all the money to be made, there was an aura of hopelessness over the city. After a time it began to premeate the soul. The straight man had yet to meet someone there who wasn't trying to make enough money to get away for someplace else. Things would happen though, and people would find themselves there, year after year. There was no cultural base to keep it together, and so the attitude was that of the South American investor: get in, make money, get out. Of course, not all could get out, and that was what shaped the character of the growing city.

The straight man had married there. He'd known many women but she'd been the only one to ever get through to him. He doubted if it would happen again. He had begun to grow soft and stupid. All those years away from the big city had dulled him, and he felt he was no longer street smart.

8/ After a while the buyers left, and the straight man and the idiot talked.

"Look, idiot, either supply these dudes or cut them loose. Don't jerk their chain."

"Okay, okay. I'll have it set by tomorrow night. No shit. You'll get your nickel and I'll get mine. It'll be a breeze. Don't forget, I'm doing all the goddamn work."

"What was the scene with Brad? Why is he involved?"

"Fuck you. You know he's okay. He took Jay for the ride. We were each gonna make a nickel if they copped, so quit bitching."

"I'm not bitching. I'm just asking what the fuck you think you're doing, that's all. If you don't do it right they're gonna get the ass and go cop in Miami. I know our prices are better. So why not get it straight and turn to them here?"

"Okay. I'll have it down cold by tomorrow. Don't worry about it."

"Man, I hope so. I really do."

The idiot left. The straight man went to bed. He thought about his ex-wife. He wondered how she was.

9/   At four the next afternoon a blue windowless van pulled up outside the straight man's apartment. He looked out the window at the van. It was unfamiliar. Ahead of it was the idiot's station wagon. Two teen-agers got out of the van. The idiot led the two long-haired kids from the van to the straight man's door. He let them in.

"Hey, man," said the idiot, "this is Jim and Tom."

"Hey," said the straight man. They all shook hands. Jim was shorter than Tom. They both had hard, narrow-eyed, southern faces. Their accents placed them somewhere in the Carolinas. The shorter of the two, Jim, did the talking.

"We got another gig tonight. The best we can do is in a day or two. We hear that y'all think these people are okay. Have you ever done anything with them before?"

The straight man shook his head. "Nope. I've never seen them before a day or so ago. My man in Chicago says they're okay. I just told the maniac here that I'd put them on to him for a nickel. That's all. It's up to y'all now. If you don't want to do the gig with these people, well, I can't do shit about it. I admit, I could sure use the dust. We all could, probably, so I hope we can do the deal. That's it."

"What do you think the chances of a rip are?" asked Jim.

The straight man shrugged. "Shit, I don't know. Moe says they're okay. I can round up some security if you want. I know some dudes that were recon marines. They're very proficient. They'd be happy to have something to do."

Jim nodded, saying nothing.

The idiot said, "I've done lots of deals like this. I know how to do it. I'll take responsibility. There won't be any problems, we'll do it right." He had a can of beer in a brown paper bag.

Jim stood up, so did Tom. Jim spoke, "Okay, we'll see what we can do. Later." They left.

The straight man looked at the idiot, "How you gonna do it?"

"I got it all planned out. We could do it at Billy's apartment. He'll be gone to the end of the month. We can stash the dope there. I've got the key. No sweat."

"Man, I sure hope you're right. I sure do."

10/ At seven that night, the cowboy hat called, "Hey, man, how ya doin'? Can you bring ten six-packs over about ten tonight?"

The straight man nodded, realized the cowboy couldn't see him, and said, "Are you at home?"

"Yeah."

"I'll call you back in five minutes." He hung up. The man immediately called the Colombo dealer's number. "Hey, man. Can I get ten from you tonight?"

"Yeah. That'll just about clean me out."

"Okay. Solid. I'll be along in a little bit. Later." He hung up. He called the cowboy hat. "Yeah, man. We're wired. See you about ten tonight. Don't fuck me up." He hung up. He made sure everything was turned off and drove to the dealer's cottage.

As he walked in he smiled, "Hey, baby, what's to it? What's goin' on?" They slapped hands like the black people did. Everyone emulated the black people.

As they settled down to smoke, the straight man said, "The idiot has some red-bud. Says he's on top of quantity. You heard anything?"

The dealer nodded, "He offered me some, but the shit isn't that good, and his price is too high."

"That's what I thought," said the straight man. "Hey, by the way, what will you front the ten pounds to me for? I had to quote a pretty low price to move it. C'mon, give me a deal."

The dealer took a deep drag. "Well, the best I can do to you for ten is one-sixty, and that's rock bottom, man."

The straight man smiled, "Okay, man. It's a deal. I'd like to put the shit in my car now, if it's okay with you. By the way, I can get grams of coke, pretty good shit, for forty-five, if you want some."

"No, man. That's too expensive, and coke goes too quick. I might be interested in an O.Z. if the price is right. None of that yellow-brown Mexican shit. It's got to be good Co-lombo, not trampled too much, you know."

"Okay, man. I'll see what I can do. What about the reefer though?"

The dealer got up, dragged the garbage bag in, set up the scale, and ten minutes later the straight man had ten pounds. The dealer looked at what remained, about half a pound, and shook his head sorrowfully. "Shit. This is what I end up with for stash." They both knew he was lying, but it was part of the game.

11/ At seven-thirty Jay and Ted came through the straight man's door. They were wearing jackets.

"Hey, what's goin' on?" asked the man.

Jay and Ted didn't look too happy about anything. "That's what we'd like to know," said Ted. "Yeah," said Jay.

They all sat down, and the straight man fired a number of Colombo. "Well," he said, "we can't do anything for a day or so. These people have another gig to do tonight. You know."

"Oh, shit," snarled Jay. "We're gonna get this static as long as we stay here. We're ready to go to Miami."

"Goddamn, man. What do you think this is, a store? You two wheel into town and expect us to jump just because you're here. You got to have patience. Five hundred pounds takes time. You ought to know that." They smoked.

"Hey, listen, can we get some coke?" said Jay.

"Yeah, but its been stepped on some. I can get you an O.Z. for about twelve."

Jay leaned forward, conspiratorily. "Do you know how much a pound costs direct from the factory? In Bolivia?"

The straight man shrugged, "How much?"

"Thirty-five hundred. That's through the cops, so there's no hassle. But they expect you to spend some money down there. You got to be careful. The factory is way out in the country. A pound looks about the size of a candy bar. One hundred per cent pure. You can step on it a few times, and turn it for ten times what it cost you."

"Sounds nice. I'd like to do that once or twice. I'd be set for life."

"There's a lot of money in reefer, too," said Jay. "I did nine months in the joint in Jamaica trying to do a deal there."

Jay was getting off on the Colombo. He grinned and continued rapping. "On the way down here we went by and visited a friend in Atlanta, Johnny Banquet. He was in charge of the air freight coming into the airport there. Every week, another shipment. Just like clockwork. I talked to him in the joint. He'll be getting out soon. Now, that was a good steady scene. We turned a lot of it for him."

"There was a knock at the door. It was the idiot, with another can of beer in a little bag. "Hi," said the idiot. "Come on. I want you to meet some of my people."

Jay looked at the straight man sharply. The man nodded, "It's cool. We're sorry about the last time. It won't happen again."

The three of them left. The straight man looked at the clock. It was time to go.

12/   Outside the cowboy hat's was a Pontiac with a Lakeland tag. The straight man remained in his car. Cowboy hat came out almost immediately, and hurried to the car. "Hey, man," he said, "Listen. I'm turning to these people for two fifteen a pound, okay?"

"Okay with me. Do they got the dust?"

"Yeah. No problem. They're a man and wife. Real good contacts."

"Okay, hat. The shit's in the trunk."

The straight man opened the trunk and carried the garbage bag into the trailer.

Inside the trailer sat the nervous couple. He was lean, nervously smiling, and wore glasses. She was so skinny that she looked emaciated. She did the talking. She probably did the thinking too. The hat was nervous too. They smoked from the garbage bag, and then she said, "Pretty good. How much?"

The straight man said, "I'm supposed to get two-twenty, but I guess we can dicker about a nickel."

She smiled, "Okay, two-fifteen. Here's the money." She pulled a leather cigarette case from her purse. Her husband kept smiling. It took fifteen minutes to count it out. One of the twenties didn't look right, and the man rejected it. Finally, the money had all been counted and the couple hurriedly moved to leave. The woman wanted to say more to the straight man. He looked at her and said, "The hat here knows how to get in touch with me." They left.

"Smooth, man. Really smooth," said the cowboy.

"Yeah. One thing though. I got to turn to you at one-ninety, so here's your share, two-fifty. Not a bad night's work. That's good shit. They'll be back, and we'll make more money."

The cowboy hat didn't argue, and happily took the money. The straight man left. He pulled into the same convenience store and transferred three hundred dollars to a different pocket. He drove leisurely to the dealer's cottage. Things were looking up.

13/ The straight man hadn't been back at his apartment ten minutes when there was a knock at his door. It was a Mexican reefer dealer. He was nervous, and excited. On occasion he'd left his scales and coke stash with the straight man for safekeeping. He dealt in anything he could turn money at.

"Hey, brother, how ya doin'?" he said as he came in. He was big, having spent many boring hours lifting weights.

"Hey, Big O," said the man. "Haven't seen you for awhile. What you been up to, or is that a secret?"

"Man, that's why I'm here. I need you for tonight. There's some people in from Orlando that want to do a deal. They ripped me on the last one, and I want to rip them back."

"Okay. How do we do it?"

"You follow me over to Louise's house, and leave your car there. I'll drop you at the Ramada Inn, and you sit tight in the bar. I'll talk them into leaving their money in the car. If the rip is on, I'll fool with my hair, like this, when I come into the bar. Then you go outside, take the car to Louise's, and leave it there."

"If it doesn't go down, you pay the cab, right?"

"Right."

"Okay, man. I hope this doesn't take all night. I'm tired, and I just did a gig. You got a spare set of keys?"

"Yeah. Right here, brother."

"Okay. Let's go."

The bar at the Ramada was crowded, but the straight man saw two rather plain looking girls seated at a table with their backs to the door. He went over and asked if he could join them. In ten minutes it was obvious that the plainer of the two was ready to hop in the sack right then.

The straight man had a clear view of the door. There seemed to be a large number of police coming in and out. He'd heard the place was hot, but this was ridiculous. He had just leaned forward to hear what the girl was saying above the din when Big O and two other guys came through the door. Big O pulled his hair in the manner agreed upon.

"Just a minute," the straight man said to the girls, "I've got to go to the men's room. Be right back." It took him nearly ten minutes to find the car in the crowded parking lot. He drove it carefully to Louise's house, locked it, got into his own car and drove home.

At seven the next morning Big O woke the straight man. He was grinning. "Five big ones, brother."

"Yeah," said the man as he began to make coffee. It was going to be a long day. Goddamn nuts that get up at the crack of dawn.

"Here's your share. Got change for a five?" Big O slapped down a bill with a picture of President McKinley on it.

"Wow," said the man. "I didn't think these things existed any more. It looks like funny money."

"It's real man, it's real." Big O hadn't stopped smiling.

"I guess it was pretty hairy there for awhile, huh?"

Big O sat down at the kitchen table. "It sure was for a while there. But after a time, I reminded them of the rip they'd pulled on me, and it's okay now. They aren't even mad."

The straight man stared at Big O. "Too much, man. Oh, by the way, here's your car keys back. And thanks for the dust, I can use it."

"That's all right, brother. This is terrible coffee."

"Fuck you," said the straight man. The sun was up, and it would probably be another hot day. His ex-wife had never made breakfast. That had been the only thing he'd liked about the Army, those big breakfasts. He sipped the coffee. It was lousy.

"You're right," he said, "this coffee tastes like shit. I should've stayed in the goddamn Army."

14/ Jay called at six that evening. "Hey, man, can your people make it tonight or not? We're gonna leave for Miami if we don't get some kind of answer."

"I told you, tomorrow night. That's the best we can do."

"Okay, man. Tomorrow."

The straight man hung up. He was bored. He called his friend's ex-wife. His friend didn't care, he'd remarried. She was home.

"Hey momma, what's goin' on?"

"Well, hey yourself. I was wondering when you were going to call me. I bought a big jar of Kama Sutra..."

"Sounds good. What time would you like to get laid?"

"I've got some people here, but they should be gone by ten."

"Anybody I know?"

"My mother and my cousin from Atlanta."

"Well, they'd better be gone by ten, or they're really gonna be surprised." She giggled, and they said goodbye.

The straight man turned on the television. He thought about writing his ex-wife another letter. She lived somewhere in the French Quarter of New Orleans. Finding her had cost money. He'd first tried to find out where she was by seducing one of her attorney's secretaries, but no luck. He'd seen faces like that secretary's peeking out of gopher holes. He turned on a cops and robbers program.

15/ At seven the following evening the blue van pulled up with the idiot's car behind it. The two teenagers and the idiot came through the door. They were all nervous. "Well, what's goin' on?" said the straight man.

"It's outside in the van," said the idiot.

"So? Now what?"

"We're going to put it in Billy's apartment. We'll do the deal there. By this time tomorrow night we'll all be rich." The idiot was grinning. Jim and Tom looked tense.

Jim said, "We met those dudes. The vibes aren't the best."

"Oh, for Godsakes, man. What do you want me to do?"

The telephone rang. It was Jay. The connection sounded distant. "We're calling from Miami. Did you people ever figure it out?"

"I'll guarantee it. What time can we expect you?"

"Shit! It's gonna take us hours to drive back there. Don't look for us until tomorrow morning, real early."

"Okay. Don't forget the money. See you then." The straight man hung up, and reported the conversation.

"Well, now we just sit tight," said the idiot.

"Let's move the shit out of the van now," said Jim, "I'm anxious."

They all went outside to the van. It had no windows. They got in and drove it down the street to Billy's apartment. It looked much like the straight man's place. In less than seven minutes they unloaded eight large white heavy canvas bales into the apartment. Jim drove the van back down the street to the man's place while the others stuffed the bales into the bathroom. They made sure the apartment was locked up tight, and walked casually to the straight man's.

The straight man turned on the television. He was getting nervous too. They all sat down and discussed the situation. It was decided that Tom and the idiot would sleep at Billy's pad with the bales. There was a phone there, the straight man could call them. Jim would sleep at the man's.

The straight man went into his bedroom for a moment, and returned with a .357 Magnum. He put it down in front of the idiot. "Security," he said.

The idiot stared at it, and waved it away. "I don't need it. I've done lots of deals like this. It's okay."

Jim and Tom said nothing. The straight man still wasn't sure. "Okay, man. Look, you want me to call a Marine friend? He got over a hundred kills in one night. He'll be glad to be security for a hundred bucks."

"No, we don't need him," said the idiot.

At midnight, Tom and the idiot left for Billy's. Jim curled up on the couch and the straight man went to bed.

16/   At four-thirty there was some violent knocking at the man's front door. As he groggily went to open it, he shook Jim awake. He turned on the lights, and opened the door. Jay and Ted, each wearing their light jackets, came through quickly and sat on the couch. The straight man called Billy's number. Tom answered. "They're here," said the man.

He turned from the phone, saying, "We got to see some money," but Jim was already leading them out the door, "to see the dope." The straight man could do nothing but follow along behind.

At Billy's place Jay and Ted quickly cut the top of each bale to make sure there was weed in each one. Jay turned to the idiot, "Where's a scale?" The idiot admitted that there wasn't one. Jay said, "Okay, we've got one in the mobile home. I'll go get it." He left.

The straight man, disgusted, went outside in the dawn knowing something was seriously wrong, but hesitant to do anything. He sat down on a cement block and watched a Chevrolet come swiftly down the street, stop, and quickly back to the front of Billy's apartment. The man remained seated on the cement block.

Suddenly Jay was out from behind the wheel and walking past him. The straight man's attention was on the car as a short, squat man with a crew-cut got out one side and a black man got out the other. Just then Jay stuck the barrel of a revolver snugly against the back of the man's head, cocking it at the same time. Jay said, almost shouting, "Federal narcotics agent! You're under arrest!"

The squat man was swinging up a sawed-off pump shotgun, and shouting, "Federal narcotics agent!" The straight man rose jerkily to his feet, putting his hands into the air.

The black man was already inside. The straight man was shoved into the apartment. He was thrown to the floor, frisked, his wallet and keys taken. Ted had covered the others from inside the apartment. Swiftly, Jim's keys were taken and his van backed to the door.

Jay walked around the living room where they were all lying, "Who is he? Who's Mister Big? I want a name! Where the fuck are the cuffs? You punks are gonna get a new asshole torn in the joint! Now talk! Use rope on these morons!"

The four were tied expertly with rope and shoelaces. Jim's van was rapidly re-loaded with the bales and driven away. Jay and Ted remained, pacing the floor, waving their guns. Fifteen minutes later the van was back. The black man and the squat crew-cut took the

Chevy and left. Jay and Ted continued to pace the floor. No one said anything. Jay took the straight man's keys and left. He returned in a few minutes. He looked at the straight man and said, "It's just a game. You win some, you lose some."

The man suddenly believed that he was about to die. He hadn't written a will. He thought of his ex-wife.

"Don't worry," Jay said, "Moe didn't rat you out." Outside, a yellow cab pulled up. Jay and Ted ran out. Nobody moved.

17/ The straight man was the first to recover. He was the first to free himself. With a knife from the kitchen, he freed the others.

The man had no feeling on the right side of his right thumb and no feeling on the back of his left hand. It took six months for the nerves to grow back. Either Jay or Ted had torn the phone out of the wall. Billy was going to be pissed when he returned. The four of them walked down the street towards the straight man's.

"C'mon," said Jim, "we've all got to go talk to the fat man." All four climbed into the van and fifteen minutes later they were at the fat man's. He listened, said nothing. Jim and Tom dropped the idiot off with the straight man. The man looked at the idiot.

"We're through, you know. Nobody is gonna front any shit to either of us when this gets out, and the importers are gonna want their investment back. You got enough to cover it?"

"Hell, no! I don't have enough money to get out of town. It's all your fault!"

"Oh, fuck you, you idiot."

The straight man called Chicago. "Moe? Hey, your friends just ripped us off for about four hundred pounds. There's gonna be some strange dudes comin' through your door soon, so if you set this up, you better tell me."

Moe said, "Hey, I didn't know they'd do that! Honest! How long we known each other? Christ, I sure didn't know. If I get a line on them I'll call you. I swear to God."

"See you, Moe." The straight man hung up. He believed him. He put his Magnum in the living room, out of sight, but where he could get to it easily.

18/ An hour later there was a knock at his door. As he opened it, seven people came through. The big one with the tattoo said, "Start talking, or we cut your fingers off, one by one."

The straight man told them the truth. He gave them Moe's address in Chicago. The gun was within easy reach, but there were seven of them. Finally, the one with the tattoo said, "Okay, we all make mistakes. We've made ours. You've made yours. You now owe us ten thousand. That's your share of the loss. You have one month to come up with the money or we'll be back, and we ain't playin' with you." They left.

The straight man watched them drive away in their Cadillacs and cursed his luck. Where would he get ten thousand? He sat down to think.

The best place to get money would probably be where they made it, the U.S. Government Mint. Nice, fresh money. The word was that if you got a job at the Mint, it was much like the casinos in Nevada, with people watching through the ceiling.

Rumor had it that at the Mint they didn't fire you for stealing. The Government psychiatrists had come to the conclusion that it was perfectly normal for someone working around all those millions every day to eventually be unable to resist temptation and steal. Supposedly, if you were a good worker they wouldn't fire you immediately, but a pink slip would terminate your employment after you'd been seen stealing a third time. That was out, it would take too long.

There's quick, heavy money in art and jewelry, but those were fields beyond the straight man's knowledge. Burglary was a field open to almost any fool, the prisons were full of them. That was out.

Kidnapping would bring in tons of Federal smoke. They had the men, the money, and the resources. If they ever got a line on you, they'd get you. That was out.

The idea of winning money gambling had built a lot of casinos. The heavy money games for the untalented were used cars and real estate. They were out, they'd take too long.

International gun running was controlled by the Spanish people and the Government. That was out.

Loan sharking was done legally by the banks for a mortgage on your soul, and illegally by the mob for a mortgage on your life. And the mob just didn't take in any dodo off the street. That was out.

Hanging paper was a possibility. With enough checks, and a good set of phony I.D., and a lot of luck, it could be done. But it couldn't be done to the tune of ten thousand with any certainty.

Cattle rustling was big business, as was moonshine. To effect entree into the moonshine business, you more or less had to be born and raised with the people in it. The pay was relatively good, ranging from a dollar to a dollar and a half for every gallon hauled.

Cattle rustling was open to everyone, some restaurants would go under without it. A cow, sans head and guts, with the hide still on, would bring five hundred dollars with no questions asked. The straight man grimaced, that was out. He wasn't about to go out in the middle of the night, cut some rancher's fence, chase some hapless cow around, butcher it and sell it without being shot down by some state patrolman or angry rancher.

Hijacking was out too, because it takes a well-organized gang for that.

The best shot would be a one-time stunt that hadn't been pulled before, like the first skyjacker. He'd thought it out and been the only only to ever get away clean. America, the straight man decided, is a nation of specialists.

The only thing the man had ever specialized in had been armed robbery. He hadn't worked for ten years, not since he'd been a punk with little respect for life. He hadn't thought about a job for a long time. Maybe a "finger" would have a line on something. He was getting too old to risk twenty years in the bucket, but he needed the money.

19/ The "finger" was a ratty man named Blaine. The straight man had done a few dope deals with him years before, and once when Blaine had been stoned he'd mentioned how he'd fingered an armored car for some people in St. Louis and gotten ten per cent of the take. He'd be the man to find. The straight man turned on the television and watched a quiz show. He wondered how long it would take.

It took three days of shooting eight ball for beer in piss-foul redneck bars before he got a line on Blaine. The man noted that his looks didn't matter to those people.

It was a warm, rainy afternoon in Tampa as the straight man pulled his compact slowly off the street and onto the asphalt that ringed the apartment complex. He carefully studied the apartment door numbers. The apartments, Florida cement block and stucco, were built to form a modified square around a large swimming pool. As the car moved along, his eye finally found the number. He continued on and parked around the corner, locking the car. The rain stopped, and the sun was bright for five in the afternoon. The apartment was on the ground floor.

The door was opened by an overripe brunette wearing a loose sleeveless blouse and too-tight shorts. She stared at the straight man with dull brown eyes, probably wondering if he was some sort of bill collector or insurance salesman. "Yeah?" she asked.

"Blaine around?"

"Yeah." She hesitantly took a step back, still not sure. He could be a cop, or a social worker.

"Tell him the straight man is here to see him."

She shrugged, "Oh, sure. Come on in," opening the door wider, still watchful.

As he walked in over the green wall-to-wall carpet of the living/dining area he was facing a sliding glass door, beyond which was the central pool area. On his left was an old couch and a scarred wooden coffee table. On the far wall hung a ragged poster of a marijuana plant. Beneath the poster was a cheap stereo. There was no furniture other than a small table with a plastic Buddha on it. To the left of the poster was a hallway that probably led to the bathroom and bedroom.

The straight man sat on the couch. He heard noises from behind a door in the hallway. There was the sound of a toilet flushing, then Blaine came through the door. He was wearing some faded beige washpants and a tee shirt. He was barefoot. He needed a pedicure. The woman had remained by the door. When Blaine saw the straight man his yellowish eyes widened for a moment, then he smiled, cautiously.

"Hey, straight man, how ya been? Sit tight. Be right back," and he hurried back down the hall.

The woman walked to the right of the sliding glass doors into what must have been the kitchen. Blaine came back down the hall with a cigar box. He set it down on the coffee table. The straight man raised his left hand, pointing toward where the woman was, and said, "Send her away."

Blaine wasn't surprised. He nodded, and called, "Hey, Sheila." When the woman looked around the corner, he said, "Hey, momma, how 'bout gettin' us some beer. Take your time."

The woman picked up an imitation brown leather purse that had been lying on the floor and stood silently next to Blaine. They didn't like each other. Blaine dug around in his pants pocket and handed her two one dollar bills.

As the door closed behind the woman Blaine grinned, showing various gaps, and fiddled around in the cigar box. "Hey, man, long time no see. I guess you heard what happened to me?"

"I heard something."

"Yeah. Got busted. Fifty pounds of two-toke Colombian in the trunk. Had every penny invested in it. I didn't talk. Had a fuckin' public defender who got me five years hard labor from a fag judge. He'd told me not to worry, I'd just get probation. Probation, hah! That asshole ought to try digging stumps sometime."

He looked up from the cigar box, smiled, and held up a nicely rolled number. The straight man took it, lit it, and inhaled deeply. First joint of the day. Tasted good.

"Pretty good shit you got here, Blaine. Tastes like commercial grade Mexican." Blaine took the number. "Right on the money, man. I got a good source." Blaine looked at the man carefully, then said, "It ought to be obvious to you I ain't holding a lot of dust, and you ain't that social, so you must be here for some reason."

The straight man took another drag, and said, "Well, Blaine, various things have happened. I need to turn some heavy dust, and I remembered a conversation we had a long time ago. You had mentioned as how you'd put some people on to a triple threat security that had paid a high rate of interest. I'm kind of in the market for something along those lines myself. I was kind of hoping you might be able to put me onto something like that. You'd get your fee, of course."

Blaine took another hit off the reefer and produced a roach clip from the cigar box. As he put the number in it, he said, "Straight man, you've always been up front with me, so I'll be up front with you. As I said, I got sent up. I did three years. I'm on parole. Reefer possession is becoming a common crime. They've been sending up little kids for it."

The straight man sat and listened. Blaine was like a dog worrying a bone. He'd get to it eventually.

"Now, where I did time at," Blaine continued, "is a place called S.C.I. That's Sumpter Correctional Institute, up in Sumpter County. My

cellmate was an old redneck in for hog rustling."

Blaine laughed, and so did the straight man.
Ridiculous. "No lie. Hog rustling. Well, anyway, one night we got high on some prison
shine and he told me a little story. Back during
the Florida boom in the late twenties he
worked on the local bank." Blaine's eyes squint-
ed to a crafty look. "Now here's the snake. He
told me about the vault. The three sides on
the inside are regular ol' steel. Heavy duty
Dieboldt time lock. All that shit. But the side
of the vault to the outside? Regular cement
block, and that's no shit." Blaine let out his
breath. It had been on his mind a long time.
Blaine leaned back on the couch. If he'd had
suspenders, his thumbs would have been hooked in them.

The man studied the marijuana poster. "You
mean that the back wall of the vault, and the
outside wall are the same?"

"That's it, man. That's exactly it. And we're
the only people that know, 'cause the old dude
died of an overdose in the joint. Say, is Jesus
still around?"

"No. He got heavy time. Tried to pull a rip
on some cats from the Treasury Department.
He'll be old when he gets out."

"Too bad. You could always cop steady from him. What's with you, anyway?"

"Nothing much. How about your woman? Does she know anything about this?"

"Man, she don't know batshit. She's from someplace up in Ohio. We've only been together a month or so. She's a good lay."

The straight man nodded. "Say some people go and investigate this. Say something comes off. What do you want out of it."

"Just my finder's fee. The usual ten per cent. If it happens, great. I'll use the money to cop reefer. I made some good contacts in the joint. Now, I got people here, and people up north, and with a few good runs, I'll be set."

"How much money in the bank there, you figure?"

"I don't know. Could go as high as a quarter of a million. Like, there's some sort of farmers' market around there every Wednesday, and all those rich orange growers. They only deal in cash, you know. Like there's the town people, and the free men out at the joint. Your guess is as good as mine. At least a hundred thou."

"Ever look at the jug?"

"Are you crazy? I left the area as fast as I could. I don't ever want to go back there, and that's no lie. No way, man."

"Okay, Blaine. We'll see. I'll be in touch. Don't get popped."

As the straight man drove slowly away, he considered the set up. If the information was up front, it was too good to be true. If the outer wall had been poured solid, that produced an additional problem. Blaine wasn't too bright, but he wouldn't talk to the wrong people, not intentionally, anyway.

The woman was another story. She acted sullen and stupid. Probably wasn't such a good lay. The backs of her legs were ripples of fat. The straight man's ex-wife had had great legs. From the way Blaine's woman acted, Blaine was going to wake up some morning with his throat cut. It was a good thing Blaine didn't want to work on this thing, because if his woman really was heavy, he'd be sated, and a sated man is slow to react. The straight man drove home. He wondered if Brad had set the rip up. He'd been with Jay long enough for them to discuss it.

20/   It was raining steadily a few days later as a late model Dodge slipped smoothly through the rutted entrance of the C&A Garage in Lakeland. The Dodge pulled onto the highway and sped away. The straight man pulled his compact quickly after it, laying back a ways. After a complicated series of twists and turns, the Dodge pulled before a small white frame house, set away from its neighbors. The driver remained inside. The man pulled next to the Dodge, and waved. The Dodge driver, known as Big Tom, studied the straight man a moment, waved back, stepped out into the rain, and scrambled to the small front porch.

The straight man splashed through the marl behind him. Big Tom had begun his career as a moonshine driver in northern Alabama. Since then he'd concentrated mainly on transporting stolen goods across state lines. He'd worked with the straight man before, they trusted one another. They stood on the rainy porch, smiling. It had been awhile.

"Hey, straight man, how you?" Hand extended.

"Fine, Big Tom, just fine. I though I'd look you up."

"C'mon in and set. Ah've got some beer in the icebox."

Big Tom unlocked the sturdy door. The inside of the little frame house could have been used in the movies. It was devoid of any personal sign. Every item in sight could be replaced from any of a hundred stores. There was a small kitchen table, with four armless plastic chairs. They sat down. Tom popped the tops of a couple cans of Budweiser. He took a swig, and asked, "Hear anything from Orloff?"

"Dead. Fouled up on an armored car in Indiana. The people with him won't be seeing the sun for long time. Wasted a highway patrolman."

"How 'bout Jackson?"

"Fat. Doesn't need to work right now."

"Little Davy?"

"Out west somewhere. How about Williams?"

"Ah heard he's swingin' a brush hook for the state. Him an' Simpson."

They looked at each other. Tom nodded. "Y'all didn't come all the way out here as a social call, did yuh?"

"Nope. I've got a job, if you're interested. It's a little odd. We may need either a ram, or some Composition 'C'."

"What are we goin' through? A wall?"

"Right, and I don't know if its been poured solid or not. All I know is that it's cement block."

"Has it been there a long time?"

The man nodded.

"Well, if it's been there a long time, it'll be almost the same as if it's been poured solid. Best way I know of, to get inside someplace, is to take a Skil saw, cut a hole in the roof."

"Tom. This is a bank. The bank's vault."

Big Tom looked out the window at the rain. It would be dark soon. He looked back at the straight man, and said, "How many people so far?"

"So far you and me, and a finger named Blaine."

"Ah don't reckon ah know him."

"I turned weed to him years ago. He got busted, did time. He's just out. You don't have to meet him if you don't want to. I think I've got most of the information we'll need. You in?"

"Ah own a piece of thet there junkyard. Borin' damn business. Where's this bank at, anyway?"

"Sumpter County."

"When do we go look at it?"

"How about tomorrow?"

"Alrighty. Ah'll be over your way 'bout ten or so."

"Okay. See you then, man."

The straight man finished his beer and left. So far, so good.

21 /   There was still ground fog at ten the next morning as Big Tom pulled up outside the straight man's apartment. The man walked out to the Dodge with a state map, notebook and pen, and a small, heavy maul. They headed north on the Interstate.

An hour later it was sunny and humid as the Dodge followed the signs down state road 61 to the sleepy little town of Sumpter. The scenery hadn't been much, the usual scattered farms, rows of orange trees, grazing cattle, an occasional cypress head. There had been no conversation.

Most of the town of Sumpter had been built parallel to the Seaboard rail line, which ran on a north/south axis. There was only one main intersection, Orange Blossom Drive. East it led to the prison. West, in the first and only block, was the Sumpter County Citizens Trust and Savings Bank. Beyond the first block were scattered old frame houses. Between the bank and the railroad tracks was a dusty-windowed Kresges. From the bank to the end of the block were three small stores, all looking worn and tired.

The Dodge pulled slowly past the bank. The vault, and a guard, could be clearly seen from the car. It was dead center in the middle of the bank. The front of the bank was faced with brick, but the little neighboring stores had only painted block. A rapid calculation in the notebook placed the center of the vault roughly seventy cement block from the corner. The Dodge slowly turned right at the end of the block. Twenty feet in from the corner was a brick alley that ran the length of the block.

Beyond the alley was an open, pie-shaped, acre-sized grassy area. It was pie-shaped because of the shell road the Dodge was now traveling over. The road curved slowly back over the railroad tracks. Directly facing the alley from across the tracks was an all-night diner. Facing the pie-shaped area and the alley from the near side were a few light green frame houses. They both studied the houses.

"How many phone lines you see?" asked the straight man.

"Ah only see one."

"Ditto." The straight man made a mark in his notebook. He said, "Okay, Tom turn around. Let's cruise down the road a ways, and we'll see what we can see."

Big Tom turned the car around at the tracks, pulled back to Orange Blossom, turned right, and drove East. Three minutes later the straight man said, "Hey, slow down. I think we've found what we need." It was an old farm, overgrown, with a large garage or barn adjoining the house. "Pull in, and let's look at it."

They drove up through the high grass to the sagging front porch. Quickly they examined the house, and then the garage, which had once been a stable. There were no locks on anything. The only item of furniture in the house was an old mattress with scattered beer cans and used prophylactics around it. The straight man nodded toward the mattress. "Poor man's motel," he commented.

"Yeah," grinned Big Tom.

They returned to the Dodge.

"What do you think?" asked the straight man. Big Tom pulled the car around before he answered.

"Well, first, if that wall's not poured solid, ah could build a ram on the front of a truck in that stable back there. The place would be a good hideout. If that wall's poured solid, Ah'm out."

"Okay. Let's go score some lunch, and then take a spin out by the prison."

"All right."

The Dodge hummed back to the town, and turned north once it crossed the railroad tracks. They had lunch at a diner an hour later in the town of Wilson. Late that afternoon they sat in the car looking at the prison.

"Boy, Ah sure don't want to go there," said Big Tom.

"Me neither. It must be hell. Seems it'd be simple to bust somebody out from the outside though. I heard about some people that did it. Walked in with shotguns, got the drop on the guards, and took some sucker right out. Real efficient."

"Yeah. Ah heard about that too. They shore musta wanted him bad. Ah don't like lookin' at that fence, and those towers."

"Me neither. Let's get out of here."

They drove away.

22/   At eleven that night the Dodge, with its lights off, pulled down the brick alley. It had begun to rain again.

The straight man was loudly counting cement block. "Fifty. Fifty-five. Sixty. Sixty-five. Okay. Stop for a minute."

Kneeling on the seat, he leaned out the window, holding the maul. Swinging it as hard as he could, he brought it against the gray wall. The block had been struck. He didn't hit a block web. The maul went in. Quickly pulling it out, he flipped back onto the seat, stuffing the maul underneath. Big Tom had turned the Dodge around by the time he rolled the window up.

"Perfect!" exclaimed the straight man. "They didn't pour it solid. We just ram through the wall, grab the dust, and split. Tom, I'm excited. This'll be a snap."

"We still got a lot of work to do," said Tom.

"Oh, hell, man. I know that. But what do you think? Easy as pie, eh?"

Big Tom grinned, "Well, so far so good. Ah'll be at that farmhouse in two nights with a truck. That'll be Wednesday night."

"Okay. I'll have the stuff, and a mace, and a train schedule."

The Dodge rolled onto the Interstate. As they rode toward Tampa Big Tom said, "How much money's supposed to be in that bank there?"

"The finger said it went from a hundred thou to a possible quarter of a million. I'd guess it's more like a hundred thou. That's a lot of oranges."

"Shore is," grinned Tom.

23/ The straight man got off the Greyhound Bus in Orlando late at night. He slowly walked the six blocks to a gas station that had long been closed. As he walked along, he hoped his friend Eugenio had really made contact with his people. It was good to have a few friends in the Cuban underground. They would do various things to earn money for their cause, but the Commies weren't known to have ever given anything back. He stopped in front of the deserted station and lit a cigarette. After a few minutes the right turn signal of a station wagon parked there flashed twice. The straight man walked to it. The two Cubans that had been sitting in it stepped out.

"*¿Eres usted el hombre derecho?*" asked one. They looked like twins.

"*Sí.* I'm the straight man. Are you Mario?"

"Yes," said the driver. The other was silent.

"Mind if I try the engine?"

The straight man slid behind the wheel. The wagon fired almost immediately. It had a full tank. "Nice touch," thought the man. He got out and walked around it. Good rubber. It had a Gainesville tag. It looked good enough.

"How hot?" he asked.

"Real hot. Very damn hot, *hombre*. *Pero* the plates are cool, man, you know?" Mario was grinning.

"Okay," said the man. He counted out three hundred dollars. "Papers?" he asked.

"No, *señor*. No papers. Papers cost a lot more, and take a long time. Eugenio said by tonight. So, it's tonight." Again, a smile.

"You two need a ride someplace?"

"No, thank you. We have another car. Good luck, *señor*. Tell Eugenio his cousin is better now. *Adios*."

"*Adios*. I'll tell him."

The straight man got into the wagon again and pulled slowly into the sparse traffic.

24/ Wednesday night the straight man was lying on the old mattress smoking a cigarette when he heard a crashing and growling of gears. A Jimmy diesel truck tractor pulled to the front of the darkened farmhouse. It stopped and backed toward the garage. The straight man hurried to the garage, pulled the doors open and waved as Big Tom backed the truck in. The station wagon was parked behind the house, out of sight of the road. Big Tom climbed down from the cab.

"Hey, Tom, any problems?"

"None to speak of. Heh, only Hertz is expectin' this thang to be in Orlando in a couple of days. Ah had to go to Moultrie to get it. Used mah last set of phony I.D. Did y'all get those I-beams and all?"

"Yep. Just like the doctor ordered. Thought the damn wagon springs were gonna bust. But I got everything on your list."

They went outside. "You can sleep in the house, or in the car," said the man. "Your option."

"Ah'll take the car, if y'all don't mind. Ah'm tired."

Go ahead. There's a pillow and a blanket there. See you in the morning."

"Alrighty."

After a while, the little night creatures began to make their noises again. An occasional car roared past the hideout.

25/ Thursday was a busy day. There were two eight foot steel I-beams and four four-foot lengths. It took them until after noon to complete the ram. The front of the truck cab looked exactly like what it was, a ram. The two long lengths extended at roughly a forty degree angle. Two of the shorter lengths were held in an X, and the other two were the supports. It drizzled all day.

The train schedule noted one train at 4:30 that afternoon. They sat in the station wagon near the all-night diner, watching it roll by.

"Ten minutes late," commented the straight man.

"That's all right. Just so the damn thang comes."

"Well, let's go down the road and cop some dinner. All that work made me hungry."

"That'd hit the spot," smiled Big Tom.

"How many minutes did it take?" asked the man.

"Ah think about four. You?"

"Same. That means we got to get in, and get out, within two minutes. With all the cops and bounty hunting volunteers in this area, it's got to be fast. I think I'd like a steak. If we fuck up, it'll be the last for some time."

They drove to a roadhouse ten miles away. The next train was at nine-thirty. The one they wanted came at one-thirty.

At one-fifteen the straight man pulled onto the road in front of the farmhouse and drove swiftly toward the town. Minutes later, he parked to one side of the shell road to the rear of the bank and building row. Pulling up his collar, he stepped out into the drizzle and hurried toward the darkened frame house that had a telephone. It took a moment to pop the phone box up and off, pull off a wire, and hurry back towards the bank alley.

When he reached the rear of the bank, he slowed, carefully scanning the dim wall and counting in a whisper. At last he found the spot. He stopped, and glanced toward the all-night diner. There was a Sheriff's deputy parked on a stool, laughing with the waitress. The man pulled a spray can of red paint from his jacket pocket, held it close to the wall, and made a large X. Clumsily wiping off the can, he tossed it aside, returned to the station wagon, started it, lit a cigarette, and waited.

After what seemed an hour, the truck ram suddenly rolled by. Tom pulled almost to the tracks on the shell road, cut his lights, and turned ponderously toward the bank. The straight man slipped the wagon into reverse, and slowly began to back down the alley, thinking how nice it would be to take a leak.

He picked up the two pillowcases, wiped his face with one, and waited. The deputy was getting another cup of coffee.

He looked toward the truck. It was moving! Too soon! There wasn't any train! The straight man scrambled from the wagon.

The truck was halfway to the wall, and Big Tom switched on its lights. The X could easily be seen. The straight man looked toward the diner. The deputy and the waitress had their heads close together. Then they weren't there. A train was suddenly blocking the view, and at almost the same time the truck ran into the wall. The wall seemed to hold for a moment, and then it disappeared.

The man ran toward the truck, which was already backing. The entire ram had gone inside. The truck lights still worked, and lit up the interior, a mass of broken block, dust, twisted steel racks, and scattered stacks of money.

The man frantically clambered over the rubble, barking his shins, calling out "steamboats." Somewhere in his past he'd been told that counting to sixty steamboats more or less equalled one minute. He'd reached fifteen "steamboats" and partially filled one pillowcase by the time Big Tom arrived. There was a trickle of blood on his forehead. Moving as fast as they could in the choking dust, they grabbed stacks of money and stuffed the pillowcases.

At the second sixty "steamboats" they stumbled outside once more. The train continued along their right. It was raining steadily. They humped to the wagon, pulled swiftly to the end of the alley, made the turn, took a turn to the right, and five minutes later closed the doors of the garage. They looked at each other and began to laugh.

26/ As they sat on the mattress sipping warm beer, counting thousands by the light of a masked flashlight, the first police car screamed by, headed toward the town. They froze when they heard it. After it passed, they continued counting.

"It's going to take them hours to sort out what happened," said the straight man, jubilantly.

"Yep. Must be a regular Chinese fire drill around there raht now. Ah'd love to see it," grinned Big Tom.

"Hey, how's your head anyway?"

"It hurts. But Ah'll be all right. We sure got a hell of a lot of fives and tens here."

"That's okay. I got nothing but stacks of fifties and hundreds here. So far I think we did okay."

Another police car howled by. During the next several hours police cars roared back and forth. They'd finished counting the money. There wasn't as much as they had expected, but it was a substantial night's work. They sat there, staring at the eighty-three thousand five-hundred and thirty dollars.

"Okay," said the straight man. "Not bad. Not bad. Here's what we do. Blaine, the finder, gets eight grand. That leaves seventy-five, five-thirty. We split that even. That gives us each thirty-seven sixty-five each. Fair enough?"

"Hit's okay with me."

They divided the money. Blaine's share went into a large manila envelope. Tom placed his split into a brown paper bag. The straight man filled the pockets of his heavy leather coat.

An hour after dawn they drove southeast, down various back roads, and got to the Interstate only a dozen miles north of Tampa. Big Tom lay in the back of the station wagon. They passed a family in a Cadillac with Michigan plates. The car radio stated that they'd gotten away with an estimated hundred and fifty thousand.

"You must not be able to count worth shit," grinned the man.

"Shit. That bank president's probably been stealin' for years. Now he can keep it."

"Yeah. You're probably right."

The man drove carefully to Big Tom's little white frame house. Tom went inside, and came out moments later. He followed the wagon in his Dodge. The straight man drove the wagon toward Tampa, and it ran out of gas almost at the city limits. After swiftly wiping it down, he carried his coat to the Dodge.

"Jesus," said the man, "you look horrible."

"Shit. Y'all ain't gonna win no beauty contest yourself."

They drove to the straight man's apartment. As he got out, he said. "See you, Tom. Take it easy."

"Why not? You too."

The straight man watched the Dodge fade away. He went inside his apartment, showered, shaved, and went to bed.

27/   The straight man didn't awaken until six that evening. He didn't get out of bed. He lay there, reviewing the previous forty-eight hours. Then, gradually, he began to have pornographic thoughts. They continued to grow in intensity. He went to his telephone and called the idiot. The idiot answered.

"Hello, idiot? This is the straight man. Can you come over right away? It's pretty important. It has to do with Jay and Ted."

"I'm right in the middle of a thing right now, man, and I have to go see some people, but I'll be there between eight and nine."

"Okay. I'll be expecting you." They hung up.

The straight man began having pornographic thoughts again, and started calling every girl he knew. There was only one answer, and she was busy. Under the letter M in his address book was a Madame's name and phone number. He called it. The Madame answered.

"Hey, Melanie, this is me. I'd like to schedule a visit with your most athletic girl for about eleven this evening. Okay?"

"Well, we just might be able to fit you in, honey."

"Okay, great. See y'all then." He hung up.

The man went to a quick food chicken place, bought the special, and returned to his apartment to watch the evening news.

Normally he watched only the international news, but today was different. He hoped there would be pictures. There weren't, but the police had all sorts of leads, and expected to arrest the culprits soon. The straight man wondered why they didn't report that an abandoned farmhouse, used by the juggers as a hideout, had been burned to the ground. They were probably tracing Big Tom's phony I.D. for the truck. Good luck, cops. The F.B.I. had been brought in. That was nice, let the incompetents take responsibility.

There was other news. Some public servant had been caught buying public lands through a dummy corporation for twenty dollars an acre. He would be allowed to resign. The international situation was normal. England was still going under, riots in Asia, and the Jews and Arabs were sniping at each other. When he thought about it, the man was always surprised that everyone wasn't just out in the street blowing each other's heads off.

28/ The idiot didn't arrive until almost ten. As he came through the door, without even checking to see if anyone else was there, he said, "Hey, I got some coke, really good nosebleed, only fifty a gram."

"Hi, idiot. C'mon in. Sit down. I got a little something for you to give those people in Cadillacs."

"Oh yeah, what? Some of my other people have a ton of Colombo."

"Shut up for a fuckin' minute, you goddamn idiot! I'm now officially though with the whole fuckin' dope scene. I'm out. From now on I'm just a user. Got that?"

"Sure, man. But this Colombo is really good shit."

"Listen, idiot. The only cat that ever had it down was the Mexican on that ship. Shit, one night me and another genius spent hours in a boat we borrowed, tooling around the bay trying to find a bale or two. You want to know what happened? I'll tell you. We didn't find batshit. We took the boat back to the marina, and as we're walking away, there's this old redneck says, 'Hey, you boys know what this is?' We go over, and you know what he'd hooked? A fifty pound bale, with lettering on it, *Producto de Colombia*. Right there, and here we are, half sick from all that bouncing around out there. We gave him fifty bucks for the whole fucking bale. He didn't even know what it was. We spent three days dryin' the shit in the bathroom, and we turned it for a buck-and-a-half a pound. Now, just don't talk to me about how much you got. You didn't know how much you had the last time."

"Yeah. Well, those people were supposed to be so fucking good. Your man, Moe, in Chicago. All that crap. And now those people want their money back."

"Money back, my ass. There was about four hundred pounds there, right? And I know cop price on the beach is maybe ten dollars a pound for quantity, so they maybe lost four grand. Plus transportation costs. Plust profit for risk. So, say ten grand tops. They were turning to the fat man for one-thirty-five, and the kids were turning to us for one-forty, and we were gonna turn to Jay and Ted for one-fifty, right? Am I right or wrong?"

The idiot nodded, and said, "Right. And they want us to each pay back ten thousand. I don't have that kind of money, so I've got to keep dealing. I don't want to deal. I just want to make enough to buy me some good cameras."

"Idiot, I wish you luck. Now, here's ten grand. Give it to those people. I don't want to see them, any of them, around here again. And if you fuck this up, I will personally blow you off, understand?"

"Wow, yeah. Where did you get the money?"

"That is absolutely none of your fuckin' business, got it? And I'll cop a gram of your coke, if it's any good."

"Oh, man. All I have with me is a taste."

"Well, fine, let me try it."

The straight man went to his kitchen and returned with a small hand mirror. The idiot pulled out his wallet and took from it a small square of tinfoil. He unfolded the tinfoil over the mirror, and the powder fell on it. When it was all out, the idiot licked the tinfoil.

"Is this shit fresh?" asked the straight man.

"It sure is." The idiot was rolling a twenty dollar bill.

"Well, if that's so, what's all this red shit in it?"

"Uh, I don't know man, but it gets you off. You'll see."

"Yeah. I'll see. What I'm lookin' at is a little coke, cut with procaine, and the red shit is meth or something." The straight man snorted it up, sat back, and waited.

Finally he nodded, "Yeah, I'm beginning to get a buzz, but not much in my throat. I think it's just meth and powder. I'll buy coke, man, but not this shit."

"Oh, man, this is good coke."

"Forget it, idiot. I ain't coppin' this shit." The straight man rose. "But don't forget to lay that dust on your people. Just don't fuck that up, okay?"

The idiot rose also, knowing it was time to leave. "Oh, sure. For sure. I'll lay it on them tonight. Sure you don't want a gram of this coke?"

"Positive."

"Right. See you later."

29/ The straight man called Moe in Chicago.

"Hello?"

"Hey, you know who this is?"

"Yeah! Two freaky characters came through my door the other night. One with a pistol, the other with a shotgun. They threatened to kill me if I didn't talk. You know what I said? I said go ahead, because you know as much as I do. I showed them where Jay and Ted used to live. Pads were cleaned out. I showed them where Jay's folks live. They went away."

"What about Jay and Ted?"

"Christ! For all I know they really could be Federal Narcs. I do know that Ted is a real gun freak. Always practicing."

"You got my number down here, right?"

"Yeah. I'll call you if I hear anything. That's a promise."

"I'll be talking to ya Moe."

"Yeah."

They hung up. It was almost eleven. The straight man went to his compact. It was time to get laid.

30/ The apartment that the hookers used was in one of the more expensive complexes. As he drove along, the man smoked a number from his best stash, which had come from a small shipment of Haitian dope that had been around a month before. He arrived at the apartment complex, found a parking place, locked the doors, and pushed the bell by the door.

A stunning long-haired blond in a sheer silken negligee peeked around the door. The straight man smiled. "Hi. I called before." She smiled, and he walked into an expensively furnished apartment. No one else seemed to be around. He sat on the couch, and pulled out his wallet. She said, "It's thirty dollars."

As he pulled out a ten and a twenty, he asked, "What's your name, anyway?"

"Paula. You want to go with me now?"

"Sure do."

She led him into one of the several bedrooms. She was nineteen, had a kid somewhere, and was very skilled. It took an hour.

As he left the hookers' apartment, the straight man took deep breaths. He felt good, but he missed the kissing, the fondling, the loving aspects of sex. He thought about his ex-wife. Jay, the fucking rip-off, or cop, might have been right when he'd said, "You get what you pay for." He got into his compact. As he drove toward Blaine's, he let his mind drift to happier times. Time to pay the finger. The envelope was in the glove box.

31/ Blaine and his old lady, Sheila, had had a fight that evening. Their problem remained the same: money. In anger, he'd slammed out of their apartment and gone to the dog track. She watched from the window as he roared away, saying venomously, "You rotten son-of-a-bitch," again and again.

She walked aimlessly around the apartment, finally turning off the lights in the bedroom. She slipped out of her clothes and lay down in bed. As she lay there, she began to softly stroke her body.

She'd left her factory worker husband in Ohio out of disgust. Florida had looked like the answer. She'd cleaned out their joint bank account, taken her car, the one Blaine was in, packed a few bags, left him a short note, and driven away. If he ever found her, he'd probably kill her.

She remembered how he'd talked her into trying mate swapping, She'd resisted the idea for months, but had finally capitulated. The couple they swapped with had a lot of experience and the whole thing had come off smoothly. After that first time, things had progressed rapidly. A few months later, she was in bed with two men when she'd looked up and seen Buck, her husband, watching her. Right then she knew she hated him.

She'd started swinging with other women. Finally, she'd been unable to take any more of it, and decided to escape to Florida. Now she was with Blaine. She moved her hand more rapidly as she went to the void. After awhile she pulled up the covers and slept.

Sheila had been asleep for several hours when Blaine came bouncing through the door. He'd been lucky, having hit the daily double three times, and a few more dollars on succeeding races. As he walked into the bedroom, he called, "Hey, Sheila! Hey momma, we're rich! Look at all this money!"

She lay there, groggily watching him pulling handfuls of bills from his pockets, carelessly tossing them on the bed. She found herself smiling. There was a knock on the front door.

"Stay put," grinned Blaine.

As he went to answer the door, she began to gather up the bills. When Blaine opened the door, the straight man handed him the manila envelope that contained his finder's fee. He immediately knew what it was.

"Hey, straight man! Thanks! Come on in. Have a beer. I just got in from the track. Heard about the thing on T.V."

"No, thanks, Blaine. I got business, you know. And I'm tired."

The straight man returned to his apartment. Blaine and Sheila made jocular love, and decided to leave at the end of the week for a new life in Denver. They rose late the next morning, and decided to breakfast at McDonalds. As they sat in her car, sipping coffee and munching on English muffins, Buck, from Ohio, walked up to the driver's side of the car, placed a double-barreled shotgun through the window, and pulled the triggers.

Within an hour the shooting was on the radio, although the name of the restaurant was suppressed. The straight man heard about it in his car, and wondered who those unfortunate people might have been.

32/ The idiot took the straight man's ten thousand to a rented house he and his ex-junkie girlfriend shared with another couple. The idiot sat on the couch, smoking a number with his old lady. He had just finished telling her about the ten thousand when he looked up and saw a man standing to the right wearing a ski mask and holding a gun. He quickly looked to the left and saw two more men standing there, also holding pistols. It was over in three minutes. The idiot had been ripped off again.

The idiot knew that when the straight man heard, he'd probably kill him. The idiot went to various dealers he knew and succeeded in borrowing nearly two hundred dollars. The next morning he began to hitchhike north.

The straight man heard that the idiot had split without paying the Cadillac people. He had heard about the robbery, but he didn't believe it. He was sipping a cup of coffee when his telephone rang.

"Hey, straight man, you gonna be home for awhile?"

"Yeah. Come on over."

"Okay. I'll be there in an hour or so."

"Okay, later."

The caller was a soft-spoken, hard-drug dealer from West Tampa, the Spanish section. The caller, normally into downs, was a Viet Nam veteran who'd shoot anyone that ever thought of crossing him. He'd seen the straight man though his changes when he'd split with his ex-wife. The man wondered what he was up to, since his friend seldom called unless the situation was serious.

"A little over an hour later they were sitting on the straight man's couch.

"Man," said his friend, "There's a buyer in town from Denver. He wants Colombo reefer. He's got a hundred thousand in cash. I've seen the money, and I was hoping we could do a thing."

"You really saw the money?"

"Yes, and the dude is nervous as a cat. He says that if he doesn't go back with dope, he'll get shot."

"Well, that sounds like horseshit. If he comes back with the money, no harm done, but I'll see what I can do."

The straight man called the dealer in the cottage. The dealer answered the phone. The man asked him to come over immediately, that it was important. He said he'd be along right away.

Fifteen minutes later the straight man introduced the middlemen to each other. No names were used. While the two dealers began to work out a way to satisfy the Denver buyer's need, the telephone rang. The straight man answered.

"Hello?"

"Well, hi there. When are you going to come see me?" It was a divorced mother of one. The man hadn't seen her in a month.

"I don't know. When would you like?"

"Bobby will be in bed in an hour."

"It'll be an hour before I can cut loose; okay?"

"Okay. Ummm. I can hardly wait." She was nice.

Back at the dealer's, the two middlemen were working out details. As the straight man listened, he flashed on a story he'd heard from a since-retired dealer. The dealer and a friend of his had filled the dealer's car with fourteen thousand worth of fronted reefer and driven it to New York to turn. They hadn't known anyone there but they'd made contact with two black dudes who'd turned every bit of it. Their profit had been seven thousand.

They had had every penny in the car, and the two spades were supposed to meet them and turn some coke to them for their trip back to Florida. They'd met on a crowded street. Suddenly there had been guns, and the two had faded into the crowd, with twenty-one thousand dollars.

The Florida dealers had been hesitant to even come back, but they had, and had been forgiven for their stupidity. The straight man would never forgive Jay and Ted. Someday he'd get a line on them.

The two middlemen had finally worked out the last detail. Both agreed to give the straight man a cut for putting them on to each other.

They left, separately. The man stuck a couple of numbers in with his cigarettes and went out. It was raining again.

33/ The only thing the straight man didn't like much about the chick, Linda, was that at her young age she had a deep worry line than ran perpendicular between her eyes. She seemed to be frowning all the time. She opened the door wearing tight gray toreador pants and a white peasant blouse. She bounced attractively when she moved. As the door closed he kissed her, and reached into her blouse from above, fondling her familiarly. She threw him a bump, pulled back with a smile, and said, "Not so fast. Wouldn't you like a drink first?"

"Sure. Let's take the drinks into the bedroom."

She chuckled, "Don't be silly. Sit down. Be good."

"I'll be good all right. I'll take a beer if you have any."

Jagger and the Stones were on the softly playing stereo. The straight man lit a number, and thought about his ex-wife. Money had been the problem.

Linda came back with a beer for him, and a mixed drink for herself. She curled up on the couch, tucking her little feet under her rear. She was beautiful. The man wondered why anyone would ever want to leave her. Of course, he'd only seen her on her good behavior. She hadn't asked for anything, yet. She took a deep drag on the proferred number.

They talked for a while. Then they went to bed. The straight man woke up in the middle of the night. He'd been dreaming about his ex-wife. He got up, dressed, and went out without disturbing Linda.

34/ The phone rang. It was a friend calling to tell him that he'd wrecked his motorcycle, broken his leg, and was in the hospital. The man teased him, wrote down the room number, and promised to visit. The sky was overcast, but there was no rain. There was a chill in the air. The straight man decided he'd drink tequila that night. Tequila was the way to escape the pain of existence.

The man rolled a few numbers, put them in with his cigarettes, and drove over to the hospital. He knew how lonely hospitals could be. The friend, Dave, was happy to see him. He was sharing the room with a black dude. The man sat down, and cranked up a number. He offered some to the black dude who said he didn't want any because he was there for ulcers. The reputed cure for ulcers, raw goat's milk, was illegal. Milk by law had to be homogenized, so a lot of people remained in pain, and the doctors kept making money.

Dave and the straight man sat in the hospital room getting high. When he left, he gave some shaved head people a ride. They stunk. The man decided to go get drunk.

35/ As the straight man walked into the freak bar, he saw James, a strange cat. James was from up north somewhere. He'd had a wife, kids, a house in the suburbs, and his own masonry company. Now his hair was long, he wore a goatee, and worked by the hour. The straight man assumed James had just given up on the middle class dream. They said hello to one another.

Behind the bar was a man named Dennis. Dennis had a college degree in something or other, had been arrested for possession, done time, gotten married, and now was the struggling artist who worked as a bartender. The other bartender also had a college degree but for some reason had no desire to do anything other than smoke dope and work in the bar. The straight man said hello to them, and ordered a draught beer.

There were other people scattered around that he knew casually. They waved, or nodded, or grinned at each other. The straight man was bored.

A brunette with a tremendous set of lungs walked up to him and said, "Hi, straight looking person." He found himself smiling at her. They'd balled a few times in the past. She'd once been married to some guy in the Marine Corps. They'd split up, and she'd been wacky ever since.

"Hey, momma, how you?"

"Well, just fine." She had an independent income from somewhere.

"Can I buy you a drink?" he asked, not really interested.

"Yes, you may," she said with a smile. The straight man bought her a glass of white wine.

Her name was Jane. She had long black hair, and a loose mouth.

"I thought you were living with that guy from Indiana," the man said.

"Oh, no. He moved out last week."

"So now you're on the town again."

"That's right. I sure am," giving him what she thought was a sexy up-from-under look.

As they looked at each other, he thought that most of the hookers he'd seen were better looking than most of the women he knew. He thought of one down in Acapulco. He and two other dudes had drifted down there once, and after getting mild sunburns on the magnificent beach, and a delicious seven course dinner, they'd climbed into a cab and said, *"Casa de puta, por favor."*

The driver had taken them around various back roads to an almost palacial residence. They asked him to wait. They walked up three twenty foot-wide steps, lit by a policeman with a flashlight, onto a gigantic patio area. From the patio one could look down on the city of Acapulco, and the ocean beyond. To the far right, snug to the building, was a conventional bar, with stools. The patio itself had scattered islands of tables and lawn chairs. They sat at one of the islands, and ordered rum cokes from the waiter.

Just as the drinks arrived, about eight or ten of the most beautiful women, dressed in evening gowns, walked up. It had taken several minutes to choose. The man had gone with a dark little fox named Sophia. She'd been worth every penny he'd spent that evening.

While they'd been in Acapulco, he'd slept with her every night. He thought about her, as he said to Jane, "Want to sit down?"

"All right. Let's sit in the other room."

They went over to where the jukebox wasn't as loud. After they were both drunk enough, he took her to his place.

36/ After he'd taken Jane home, the man returned to his own apartment. He looked at his bed with distaste. He thought about his ex-wife. He took a shower, then called the dealer in the cottage, but there was no answer. He didn't even feel tired. He dressed and decided to go out and really tie one on.

The beer and wine bars closed at one, so he went to a liquor bar. Their licenses were good until three. He went to a bar that had one of the most unsavory reputations in town. It had changed in the last few years, and now was a cheap, topless, rip-off type place. He sat there, watching the naked, part-time hookers.

By three o'clock he still wasn't drunk enough. He drove to a bottle club that stayed open until five. At the bottle club he knew he was drinking moonshine that had been colored with tea. He didn't care. A pool hustler challenged him to a game of eight ball, for a drink. He accepted, and slop shot himself to victory. The hustler was positive he had a fish.

The straight man bought him a drink, and talked with a burly fellow who'd been in prison in Michigan. For a while they discussed safes. They both agreed that the easiest safe was a Kent, and the most problematical was a Dieboldt, because, depending on the year of manufacture, the box location was different. A Mossler was a good safe, but the locking bar that runs between the dial and the handle could always be cut.

They were both a little drunk, and had a long argument as to whether a Dieboldt should be peeled from the left, or the right. The straight man remained positive that it was Dieboldt from the top left, and Mossler from the top right. He got home to his apartment at five-thirty, drunk enough to sleep.

37/ At about nine that morning someone was beating on his front door. Wired from booze and lack of sleep he opened the door and admitted the dealer from the cottage. The dealer ate nothing but health foods and seldom drank. He always rose early.

"Hey man, how you doin'?"

"Oh, groovy, man. Just groovy." The straight man felt as if the Russian Army had marched through his mouth, whistling.

The dealer was all smiles as he plopped himself onto the couch and chattered away as the man put on the coffee. He continued talking as the man went into the bathroom. The inside of the toilet was ringed with what looked like old vomit. The straight man couldn't remember being sick when he'd gotten home. When he came out of the bathroom, the dealer was just in the process of lighting a pipe filled with some sort of black hash. The dealer grinned at him, and fired the pipe.

"Hey, brother, sit right down and toke on this. Finest elephant ear hash in the United States, direct to you from Afghanistan."

The straight man sat down, and said, "Man, I sure hope it's good, 'cause I was drunk as a lord last night, and probably made a total fool of myself."

"Toke up brother. Just toke up. This'll cure what ails you."

The dealer rose, and took care of the coffee. The straight man smoked the hash. It was the greatest. They both sat there, happily out of their minds until almost noon, at which time the dealer suggested that they go to lunch at a health food restaurant. The man agreed.

Still partially high, they had large salads with sour cream dressing. They had almost returned to the straight man's apartment when he had that first feeling of queasiness, and the foreknowledge of impending sickness.

Five minutes after they'd arrived at his apartment, he was on his knees in the bathroom. The dealer said goodbye, and split. After he'd thrown up the third time, the man knew he was going to die soon, and wished he'd written his will. He didn't leave the bathroom. He just lay on the cold tile floor, dozing, waiting for death. After he threw up for the fourth time, he swore he'd never eat health foods again. He wished he'd written final letters to his family.

Sometime that night he crawled to his bed. The next morning he was weak as a kitten. He tottered when he walked, but he was relatively sure that he'd survive.

He cooked some beef bouillon, for survival purposes. The day drifted by. His one black friend in town called, and said he'd bring some hamburgers when he came over. The straight man told him to make sure that his hamburgers had absolutely no condiments on them, just plain bread and meat. The friend was true to his word. The man moved as if he were a hundred years old. They watched television.

The straight man went to bed early. It was raining outside. He considered suicide, something he hadn't done since he split with his ex-wife. He had no dreams.

He woke before dawn, looked around, and went back to sleep. He woke again about nine, in a sweat. He'd been kissing his ex-wife, and she was an armadillo. He got up and took a shower, then went to a pancake house and had a large breakfast. He was well again.

38/ As he sat eating pancakes and link sausages, he watched a 1951 Ford drive past. He remembered many years back when he'd had everything he owned in a '51 Ford, including a pound of cocaine. He'd left Gainesville about seven in the evening, bound for Chicago. The car had never caused any problems previously, but about midnight the car had suddenly ceased. The temperature gauge was registering "hot."

He'd coasted slowly over a low hill and into a gas station that must have been built about 1920. He stopped at the old-fashioned, glass-topped pumps. A friendly old fellow named Randall had poured water into the radiator, and they'd both stood and watched it flow out the bottom. The straight man had been sweating, because he'd only had about thirty-five dollars on him. The car would still run, but the radiator was shot. Randall insisted that he could weld the radiator. The man didn't believe it was possible, but helped pull it.

Backed into the bushes next to the station was an old flat bed tractor trailer loaded with sacks of potatoes. Occasionally, the tractor would start. Randall volunteered the information that the driver was in there with some woman. After awhile the driver, a tall skinny man with greasy black hair, came from the tractor to get a couple of cups of coffee. The straight man spoke to him, and found out the man was supposed to be in Terre Haute, Indiana. Further conversation revealed that he was a week late already, was coming from

Lake City, only a few hours to the south, and didn't much care if the straight man took a sack of potatoes. The straight man took a twenty pound sack. He never saw the woman.

After nearly an hour, Randall admitted failure. The radiator now looked as if someone with a .22 had been using it for target practice. Randall was an optimist. He suggested they go to a boneyard, and the straight man could get another radiator. It seemed a good idea, only there were additional problems. The man who owned the boneyard would shoot them, unless the Sheriff accompanied them over there.

The Sheriff wouldn't go with them unless he was given a drink. Randall didn't have any juice, and the "government" whiskey store was closed. It was now two a.m. Randall was positive that he knew where they could get some moonshine. He went over to the truck tractor, and asked the driver to keep an eye on the station.

Randall started his car, a '52 Buick convertible, the top nothing more than the frame and a few scraps of the original rag. The straight man threw the sack of potatoes in the back seat, and off they went through the foggy Georgia night.

In minutes the straight man was lost. After a time they drove down a dirt road to an old two storey frame house which had every light on. Randall parked at the front door. There were no other cars to be seen. The straight man carried the potatoes to the wide porch. Randall led the way, and beat on the door. It was opened by an incredibly fat black woman. She and Randall seemed to have known each other a long time. In less than five minutes the fat woman had the straight man's potatoes, Randall had a cup of moonshine, and the man had a large mason jar of corn whiskey.

Again they bounced through the night. Randall's driving seemed to have improved. After a time they came to a small stucco house with a manicured lawn. The straight man stayed in the Buick, listening to the rods, while Randall went to the house. After about fifteen minutes the Sheriff came out, strapping on a gunbelt, and talking to Randall. The straight man moved to the back seat. Never once during that incredible evening did the Sheriff ever seem to notice him.

They got into the car, and both Randall and the Sheriff began to have a taste of the contents of the mason jar. The boneyard was dimly lit by two bulbs on telephone poles. By way of introducing their arrival, the Sheriff pulled out his .44 Special, pointed it in the general direction of the sky, and squeezed off a round. A light came on in a shack in the middle of the boneyard, and a grizzled old fellow welcomed them with a toothless grin, and a double-barreled shotgun. All four of them entered the shack. The straight man even had a taste.

After a few tastes he found himself wandering alone through the junkyard with a Boy Scout flashlight, looking for a radiator. After succeeding in getting filthy, the man found a radiator that looked like it might work. He returned to the shack, where the good old boys were eating goobers, having tastes, and gossiping. The radiator cost ten dollars. The mason jar was empty. Happily waving good-bye, they roared back to the Sheriff's house. Randall's driving demonstrated his intention to enter the Firecracker 500 the next July.

At last they returned to the gas station, and the straight man tested the radiator. It held water. They began to install it. It took some time. The tractor started once. Dawn was in the offing, and the cattle across the road had begun lowing. At last it was time for the great test. The Ford started and the radiator held. Randall wished him luck, and the straight man was back on the highway.

South of Macon, Georgia, is a forest preserve. It was a bright, warm morning when the Ford stopped running forever. The straight man, tired, stubbled, his eyes full of sand, locked the car, raised the hood, and leaned on a fender with his thumb out. He was given a ride almost immediately by three men on their way to work in Macon. They dropped him off at a gas station just south of some railroad tracks that crossed one of the town's main arteries.

The man knew one name in Macon, but an examination of the telephone book revealed perhaps thirty people with that name. The gas station owner was busy, and in a distracted voice said that he'd send a boy with a truck and chain to tow the Ford in, for fifteen dollars. The straight man agreed. After bouncing along with a nervous black man for about twenty minutes, they arrived at the car. It hadn't been touched, and they towed it back to the station.

The straight man now had ten dollars cash, a car with a frozen engine, everything he owned, and a pound of cocaine. He felt miserable, so he had some breakfast in a cafe across the street. After he finished he walked back over to the station and told the owner he could have the Ford for fifty bucks. The owner said thirty-five. The straight man took it.

The man's possessions were in one large pile on the sidewalk. He found that he could carry half the pile at a time. Various people watched amusedly as he moved his things half a block at a time. Six trips, and three blocks later, he arrived at the Greyhound bus terminal, where they informed him that he had enough money to either ship his things or himself, but not both. The straight man chose to ship his things, which cost about twenty dollars.

Keeping one small bag containing some underwear and his shaving kit, he began to hitchhike toward Chicago. Two days later, outside the town of Calhoun, Georgia, he was so frustrated and cold that he threw empty beer cans from the roadside at passing police cars. A warm jail with meals would have been nice. The police were unsympathetic, and they ignored him. Finally, in desperation, he got a motel room, showered, shaved, and resolved to get out of Georgia the next day.

At ten the next morning, while standing at a street light in downtown Calhoun, he saw a Pontiac with Illinois plates. He ran up to the car and asked the solitary driver for a ride. Late that night he was let out in southern

Illinois, at the intersection of two roads. That was all. There was nothing to be seen in any direction. Toward dawn a master boiler maker from Chicago gave him a ride into the city.

Each day he'd called Greyhound about his things. After two weeks of calling, he finally was able to do a coke deal. The coke had been in thermos containers, surrounded with rice, and had been as fresh as when it was packed. As the straight man watched the Ford through the window, he smiled at the memory. He finished his pancakes and returned to his apartment.

39/ The phone rang. It was Glen, a strange Norwegian.

"What you been up to, straight man? I've been trying to reach you."

"Nothing much. Went on a drunk. I'll never drink again."

"Uh-huh. I've said that once or twice myself."

"What about yourself?" Glen worked for the telephone company, and made some spare change by selling lids at work.

"Oh, this and that. Need a carbine?"

"Carbine? Are you shitting me?"

"No lie. Comes with a thirty round banana clip. Real accurate, only a buck-and-a-half."

"No, thanks. I'm not in the market right now. If you get anything else, let me know."

"Okay, man. Got any good shit?"

"No. I'm out of the scene, entirely."

"Well, hang in there."

"You too."

The straight man mused, "Carbines. What next?" He took his laundry out. He was feeling better every minute. When he returned, the phone was ringing. He leaped to answer it. It was the cowboy hat.

"Hey, straight man. There's a big party out at the fish farm Saturday night. It's Sammy's birthday. You gonna be there?"

"Yeah. I'll probably be there. First time I heard about it. Thanks for telling me."

"Good. There'll be a couple of kegs, and some oysters. There's supposed to be a band, too."

"I'll be sure and be there. What else is new?"

"Nothing much. Somebody got popped with a semi full of reefer. Know anything about that?"

"Nope. How much did they have?"

"I don't know. The news said it had a street value of half a million, so it was maybe worth forty or fifty thousand."

"Yeah. The cops must figure it by the number. That's one I knew nothing about."

"By the way, I heard Ralph is back in town."

"Oh yeah?"

"Yeah. I haven't seen him yet. Listen, man, I got to go."

"Thanks for the call, hat."

"Yeah. Catch you later."

They hung up.

So Ralph was back in town. He was a strange one. His experience in Nam had given him a radical political conscience, and he'd organized a few anti-war demonstrations at the local campus. One night he'd been driving home, drunk out of his mind, and run into a group of mailboxes. One mailbox had remained on the hood of his car, and he'd been awakened the next morning by the police. The Government prosecuted him under some mail statute and sent him to prison. The man wondered if Ralph would keep his mouth shut now.

A cat named John had been sent up about the same time as Ralph. John was a real skinny guy who lived off fruit juice and reefer. He'd decided to try his hand at smuggling. He'd driven to Texas, copped about fifty pounds, which was all he could afford, and driven it back to Florida. When he'd reached Tampa, he'd been pinched. The Treasury Department had been on his tail the whole way. He'd been sent to prison. The irony was that he'd have only made about five hundred after expenses. The straight man shook his head. What was he doing handing around with these airheads?

40/ There was a knock at the door. It was a car scavenger and sometime burglar named Jerry. He was part Indian, had very large eyes, and was much younger than the man.

"Hi, Jerry. How's the car business? Score any brand new Continentals recently?"

"Fuck you, straight man," grinned Jerry.

The straight man began to roll a number. "Well, what's up? How do you get your cars, anyway?"

"We drive around until we see a car that oughta be junked. Then we see if we can get it for free, or maybe five bucks. Then we got to break out the windows, pull the seats out, and put a hole in the gas tank. I can get maybe twenty to forty cents the hundredweight. Depending on who I take it to."

"That ain't bad money, for a nut."

Whenever Jerry got caught doing something, he'd act crazy, and the authorities would send him to the state mental facility at Chatohoochee. After about six months there, he'd be declared cured, and released.

The straight man and Jerry toked the reefer. Finally, Jerry got around to speaking what was on his mind.

"Man, you know anything about checks?"

"What kind of checks?"

The man had turned a few thousand in shoe company checks once, when he'd been in high school. He'd been selling phony I.D. in those days. That was a lucrative period, B.D., Before Drugs, when drinking was still in vogue. One of his associates in the I.D. business had driven to Georgia and come back with several thousand blank driver's license forms. All that was needed to validate the blank was the state stamp, which was the outline of the state. Using tracing paper, the straight man had lightly pencilled it in, then used a pen and a comb over the outline to create the official looking cerrations. They'd sold separately for ten dollars.

Birth certificates were purchased from a worker at the county hospital for a dollar apiece. Putting on the baby's footprint had been done by making a fist over an ink pad, outer edge of the hand down. The toe prints had been the little finger's pad, five times. Those had sold for twenty apiece. A few more cards, all with the same name and description, had created a new identity. Then everyone could go drinking.

Using various identities, in a two day period the group had cashed checks all over the state and never been caught. High school had been an exciting time.

He looked at the stack of certified money orders, all in blank, that Jerry had tossed on the coffee table. "Have you used any of these?" he asked.

"No. I don't know how to do it. What do I do?"

"Well, first you score a checkwriter. That's a little machine that stamps whatever amount you want to write it for. You use a typewriter for the rest of it. Then you need a set of phony I.D. You make the checks out for weird de-nominations, never an even number, like two hundred thirty-seven eighty-two.

"Now comes the hard part. A bank will bust you, normally. So, what you've got to do is go to some other town and look in the paper for people selling shit. Say there's an ad to sell a diamond ring for two hundred. You call 'em up. You wear a suit and tie. You cop the diamond with your phony check, and a couple bucks too. Always go over to cop after the banks are closed. You get change, maybe something else as well. You leave town. If you cop on a weekend, then score other shit, like stereos, televisions, coins. You take all the shit to another town and pawn it. That's how it's done."

"Hell, I couldn't do all that. You could. You look right."

"Well, that's how its done, Jer. I've done it before. I won't do it again. Somebody might be interested in copping the checks, though. How much you want for them?"

"I need three hundred."

"Well, I'll tell you what. If I find anyone in the market willing to pay the price, I'll leave a message at that number you gave me."

"Okay, man." Jerry gathered up the checks, stood up, and at the door raised his fist in the Socialist salute. Everybody was political. "Later," he said.

Strange cat, that Jerry, thought the man. He'd been married once, and after his ex-wife had gotten through with him he hadn't cared what happened to himself. One night he'd come over with a sack of quarters, to see if they were worth more than face value. They weren't.

The straight man rolled a number. He thought about all the screwed up people he knew. Every one of them had started out okay, but somewhere along the line they'd fallen in love, and if it hadn't worked, they'd become fucked up. Every lonely man sitting in a porno movie was there because of a woman somewhere. It might have been their mother, or sister, or wife, but somewhere along the road they'd been burned. The straight man refused to think about his ex-wife.

He called a woman who'd introduced him to Greek culture. As he picked up the phone he wondered if he had a Don Juan complex, whatever that was. There was no answer. He decided to go visit a weight lifter friend he hadn't seen for awhile. He went to his car.

41/ Mike was home. He lived in a tiny duplex that he kept spotlessly clean. The straight man walked in.

"Hey, big fella, how you doin'?"

Mike was morose. "Not so good, man. Not good at all. My car is busted, transmission's gone. Cindy went back to North Carolina. I've been out of work for three weeks and I'm supposed to pay the rent tomorrow. I don't have the money. I don't know what the fuck I'm gonna do." He pulled his goatee. He was really down.

"The man nodded sympathetically. "Things don't sound so hot. You could always sell your stereo. How about that?"

"Without music I really would go crazy. I know of a deal though."

The man assumed a blank expression.

Mike was just a nice, regular guy. With a steady job he was the salt of the earth. He was proud to be a member of the Laborers Union. He liked using his considerable strength tying steel, setting snap-ties, and all the rest of it. He and the man had met on a construction job. The man worked occasionally to keep any possible normal heat from looking too closely. Most people, given a job and made to feel useful and of some importance, were generally content. But when it isn't there, when the financial pinch begins, when love walks out the door, then people start to get freaky. Mike was about there.

He went to the kitchen and came back with two large glasses of Kool-aid over ice-cubes. The straight man took a big swig. "Okay," he said, "Let's hear it."

"Well, I can butt a pound of hash from The Gunman. You know him?"

"I've seen him around once or twice."

"Yeah. I can get a pound from him of good stuff, for nine hundred dollars. I could ounce it up and make a big profit."

"You ever do anything with him before?"

"I'm not worried about a rip-off."

"Is the hash gonna be any good?"

"Oh, yeah. He gave me a taste. It's in the bathroom. I'll go get it." Mike rose, and hurried off.

The Gunman got his name when he was working in a liquor store. Some smart ass tried to hold it up, and in the shooting that ensued The Gunman had taken a bullet in his spine. He was condemned to a wheelchair forever. The holdup man had never been caught. Mike returned. They smoked the hash. It was excellent.

"You hear about Mad Melvin?" asked Mike.

"No. I don't know any Mad Melvin."

"I don't know him very well either. But I heard he talked to the cops, and the people he talked about are gonna cut his legs off at the knee."

"Remind me never to talk to a cop, even when I'm getting a ticket."

That was the kind of story the man could go without hearing about. He decided to loan Mike the money. "What would you say if I said I'd front you the dust, interest free, for one week?"

"I'd say that you'd be about the nicest mother-fucker I knew. Man, are you really serious?"

"Yeah. The money is in the bank. I'll go get it tomorrow. You'll have it by tomorrow evening. It's for one week. If I don't have it back by then, I charge you interest. If you split with the dust, I'll blow you off."

"Oh, man, thanks, man. I won't split. You'll get your money back. Is there anything I can do? Anything, man. Want me to suck your dick? Go shoot somebody?"

The straight man laughed. "Just don't fuck up, Mike. Listen, while I'm feeling so good, I think I'll go out and see if I can scare up some pussy. You be here tomorrow afternoon, for sure."

"For sure. For sure. I'll be here. Jesus, thanks, man. Goddamn, I don't know what to say."

"You just straighten your act out with The Gunman."

"Yeah, sure. Whatever you say. I'll be here, man, and I'll talk to The Gunman. Thanks again, man."

"Later."

42/ As the straight man pulled away from Mike's broken car, he thought about Mike and Cindy. She'd been a cute little blonde. Had some small scars on her face. He thought about his ex-wife. He decided on a whore, no involvement. He drove toward Tampa's strip, Dale Mabry.

He pulled into the parking lot of a nightclub famous for its hookers. He sat by himself at the bar, ordered a vodka martini, and looked the whores over. There were several very beautiful ones. He finally chose one seated on the other side of the bar. She looked like a movie actress that had gone blind in one eye. He asked the bartender to buy her a drink. He also told the bartender to tell her he wasn't a cop. She accepted the drink, smiled, and gave him the "come hither" look. He rose, walked around the bar to her and slid onto an adjoining stool. Without looking at him she said, "You want to come out? It's fifty dollars."

He looked her over. She was wearing red hot pants, and she had excellent legs. "You got a deal." he said. "Is it okay if we finish our drinks first, or you in a big rush?"

"I don't care. My name's Denise. What's yours?"

"Mike." He smiled. "I'm a laborer."

They finished their drinks.

"You ready?" she asked.

"Lead the way, momma."

They went outside. It was still daylight. She said, "You got a car?"

"Yeah, over there." He pointed at his compact.

She unlocked the door of a Chrysler and said, "Follow me."

He went to his car, started it, and waited. She pulled past without a glance. They drove three blocks to a cheap motel. Without a word she led him into a room with two double beds. He closed, and locked the door, pulled out his wallet, and tossed a fifty on the decrepit dresser. He walked between the beds and began to undress. She took the bill, put it in her purse, and began to strip. She was nude before he was. She had a good body.

"Do you want a blow job, half and half, or a lay?"

"Half and half," he said, as he lay back on the bed, eyes closed.

An hour later he was back at his apartment.

43/ He'd just turned on the evening movie, and put nine bills in an envelope for Mike, when the phone rang. It was one of the Cadillac people. The straight man told him he'd given his share of the loss to the idiot.

"The idiot got ripped again, and left town," said the Cadillac man.

"Well, I gave him the money. That's no lie, and that's all I could raise. So take it out of his hide, not mine."

The Cadillac man said he'd be in touch. The man made himself a cup of coffee. He'd never seen the movie before, and was thoroughly involved in it when there was a knock at the door.

He kept watching the movie as he opened the door. It was the dealer from the cottage, wearing white pants and a white knit shirt.

"C'mon in. Don't say a word. Ever see this movie?"

They sat down. The dealer pulled out a number. They smoked and watched the movie. At the commercial the straight man turned to him, smiled, and said, "I'm never gonna eat health foods again."

"Yeah. You sure were sick. You know it wasn't the health foods?"

The man laughed. "How ya been? That Denver deal ever go through?"

"Sure did. Everything went like clockwork. Turned six hundred pounds to them at one sixty-five. Didn't make as much money as I'd have liked to. Your friend and I split the fifteen profit."

"How much was that?"

"Nine grand. So we figured we'd each give you five hundred for putting us on to each other. Here's the money."

He pulled an envelope from his underwear, took out ten one hundred dollar bills, and laid them on the coffee table. The straight man picked up the money, folded it once, and stuck it in his pocket.

"Thanks, man. I can sure use the dust. The idiot has left town."

"Yeah. I heard that tonight. I also heard that he got ripped for a bundle, and that it was your money."

"That's right. But it's a small world. We'll see each other again some day. Want a beer?"

"No, thanks. My old lady is out in the car. I just took her to dinner. I better take her home."

The movie was coming on again. "Okay, thanks," said the straight man. "See you soon."

44/ The door hadn't closed behind the dealer when the phone rang. It was the other dealer. "Have you seen your friend?" he asked.

"Yeah. He was just here. He laid some bread on me."

"How much?"

"One big one. Was that right?"

"Yeah. Thanks again, brother. I needed that one."

"No sweat. Listen, I'm tied up right now. Talk to you later, okay?"

"Okay, man. Thanks again."

The straight man hadn't made it back to the couch when the phone rang again. Another commercial had just come on. He was irritated, and answered the phone gruffly, "Hello!"

"Well, hello there. Don't bite my head off." The Italian chick.

"Hey, momma. What's up?"

"Would you like to come over?"

"Are you wearing any clothes?"

"Yes, why?"

"Well, why don't you slip over here? I'm watching a movie on TV called Z."

"What does Z mean?"

"I don't know. I've been on the goddamn phone all the time. C'mon over."

"Okay. See you soon."

The commercial was just over. Fifteen minutes later the Italian chick came in wearing shorts, a blouse, and sandals. She had a little suit on a hanger and a pair of shoes in her hand. "For work tomorrow," she smiled.

He grinned at her, gave her a big kiss, and sat down in front of the movie.

"I see you put on clean sheets," she said.

"Yeah. Take off your clothes. The movie will be over soon. Want a beer? Here, roll us a number."

He handed her a baggie full of marijuana. There were several decks of papers scattered on the coffee table.

When the movie was over, he said, "Let's go take a shower."

After drying off they went into the dimly lit bedroom and lay on the sheets, smoking a final reefer, allowing their awareness of each other to heighten. The man had a difficult time conjuring up a clear image of his ex-wife, so he let it alone.

45/ She got up and left without disturbing him much the next morning. He lazed in bed. He considered what he ought to do. Maybe he ought to go to Miami for a few days, get away from all this shit for awhile. He knew some people there, down in Coconut Grove. Finally, he got up, threw on a pair of faded jeans and a tee shirt, and walked into the bathroom. When he came out he picked up the envelope for Mike. He decided that if he went to Miami, he'd miss the party at the fish farm. Few dealers ever went to those parties.

Mike was home, and almost jumping up and down with excitement. "Man, oh man, oh man. I talked to The Gunman. The deal is on for six o'clock tonight!"

"You seem to be pretty excited. Here's the dust. Now remember, don't fuck up, or I'll have to call the Mafia."

"Oh, man. I won't fuck up. I've got a couple ounces sold already. You'll get your money back in less than a week. I promise."

"Okay, okay. Just calm down. Don't let The Gunman con you. Make sure you're getting weight, 'cause if it's light count, it's money out of your pocket."

"Oh, I know, I know. I'll do it right."

"Okay. You got the dust. You're on your own. I wish you luck."

They shook hands, like bankers. As the straight man drove away there was no doubt in his mind that he'd get his money back. He drove to his bank and made a car payment.

46/ It took Mike four days to pay the straight man back. He'd sold the hash for a hundred an ounce. He was elated about it all.

"Tell me," said the man, "did you weigh it?"

"Not until I got back home. I was supposed to lay the dust on The Gunman. Then we went and sat by the street. A car came by, and the exchange was made. He came back with it, and I took it home. It was thirteen grams light."

"That's about half an O.Z."

"It was worth it to me, man. I paid the rent, and my car's in the shop. I'm supposed to get it next Tuesday. I paid you back, and I've got money in my pocket. Hey, do you know Big O?"

"Yeah. What about him?"

"He seems like a real up-front character."

"He is."

"Did you go to that party out at the fish farm?"

"Yeah. It was great. I didn't see you out there. Were you there?"

"No. I stayed home. I sold six ounces that night."

"Oh, yeah. There was quite a bit floatin' around that night. All the local crazies were there. There was a band. The cops came. I was pretty fucked up by then, and I asked one of the cops for a cigarette. Said he didn't smoke. I turned a cop on once, y'know. He got high and was rolling around on the floor. You know what he said? He said, 'Man, you're the only dude I trust myself to get drugged with.' "

"Man, I borrowed this dude's car. I got to go."

"Hang in there, Mike. Don't get popped."

As the straight man watched the Volvo pull away, he saw one of his strangest friends, Sam, coming toward the apartment on his only possession, a bicycle. Sam had had a waterbed store once, and then he'd met some woman who screwed him up somehow. He'd sold his business, and spent all the money on drugs. He lived day to day. A very personable guy, but hopeless. The straight man let him in, they smoked dope, and watched T.V. After the evening movie, he left. He was back banging on the door almost immediately.

"Hey, man. My bike's gone!"

"You sure?" They went outside. It was gone all right. The straight man considered what to do.

"Well, I'll try and get it back for you. The little kids around here are ripping them off left and right. I'm friendly with one of them. I'll see what I can find out. Why don't you take my bike in the meantime? I don't use it anymore, and you need the transportation. Here, take it. By the way, it's hot."

"Yeah. Thanks, man. Later."

"Later."

The next day the straight man made inquiries of the little kids. They all denied knowledge of anything. The following day Sam called. "Hey, man?"

"Yeah."

"You know what?"

"What?"

"Somebody ripped off your bike last night."

The straight man laughed so hard his stomache began to hurt. "Don't worry about it, man." He hung up.

A rip-off world. Once he'd worked in a bar in Chicago. On Saturdays he'd drive to Indiana to buy booze for the bar. There hadn't been a sales tax in Indiana. The juice had been poured into the bottles with the Illinois tax sticker. The waitresses had been part-time hookers. There had been a pair of bookies. One of them would sit in the bar all day, nursing Martinis, and by evening was still sober. Then his partner would come in. He'd spent his whole day in a room somewhere, taking bets. He'd give the collect and pay list to the sober one. He'd have about three drinks and be out of his mind. They'd both been tailors once, and had all sorts of pockets. It had been an interesting bar, probably owned by The Mob.

The Mob. The man had recently been to a party hosted by a Spanish attorney. It had been attended only by nice, elderly men. The man had a few drinks too many, and chancing the title of "smart ass" had pointed out to a friendly giant that they really ought to worry about things like pollution.

The giant had looked at him seriously, and then said, "You know who ought to take care of all this pollution crap?"

"No, who?"

"The Mafia, that's who."

"How do you mean?"

"Say some big corporation, with a lot of attorneys, is polluting like crazy. The government can't do shit. Now, a couple of the boys drop in on the corporation president. You bet, there'd be results."

It would probably work, thought the straight man. The Mafia ought to go public. They could take care of the crooks, and the cops could keep busting the citizens.

47/ The phone rang. It was the Norwegian, Glen. "Hey, straight fella, guess what I got?"

"The clap? A tank? A cannon?"

"An elephant gun. Really heavy duty."

"What the fuck would I use it for? There aren't any elephants runnin' around outside, and I'm not going after any armored car in the near future. I'm beginning to think you're fuckin' nuts."

"You sure you don't want it?" Glen sounded hurt.

"I'm positive. I'll tell you what I really need though. I need a one fifty-five millimeter cannon. Self propelled type. I'm gonna use it on the Federal Building downtown. I'll need lots of ammo too."

"You sure you don't want it? It's really a beaut."

"Keep in touch, Glen."

The straight man wondered what was going on. He'd been in one place too long. It was starting to get to him. Too many people knew where he lived. Too many loose remarks on the telephone. He'd even been ripped off. He'd never had a telephone before he'd come to Florida. He'd been careful before. Out of the old days he'd only kept in touch with Moe up north, and Big Tom down here. The time in the Army had made him step away, and his ex-wife had made him soft. Christ, he'd even had a bicycle. He laughed. A bicycle. If he didn't get out of town soon, it was really going to be all over.

It was time to go. He'd gotten what he could from Florida. He had over thirty thousand. He had a valid passport. He'd never been arrested, except once for swinging on a cop. The cop had had it coming. He'd been one of those lean, nasty bastards. The man had been sitting in a restaurant for over an hour when the cop had come in, taken him out, and begun to give him a speeding ticket. The man knew he hadn't been speeding. The cop admitted he hadn't clocked him, nor given chase. That's when the man swung on him. He hadn't seen the cop's partner. He still believed the cop had had it coming. After he'd told the judge what had happened, he was fined twenty dollars. It still rankled. He knew he had to get out of town, out of the state.

The phone rang. It was Moe, in Chicago. "Hey, man, I got some news for you."

"Bad news travels fast. What is it?"

"This is good news."

"Well, run it."

"I got a line on Jay and Ted."

"Tell me all you know, I got a minute."

"They sold your dope in Pennsylvania, er, the capital city there."

"Scranton."

"Yeah. Well, anyway, Jay has a sister. Lives out in Wheeling. Through a girlfriend of hers, who happens to know my old lady, I found out where they are."

"Where?"

"San Francisco."

"You got an address? Anything like that? That's a city."

"No address, but Jay is using the name Xenos. Ted's there too."

"How you spell it?"

"X-e-n-o-s. That's all I know, man."

"Yeah. Thanks. This is a personal matter. Don't mention it."

"Okay, man. This call is costing me. Sorry about them."

"No sweat, man. You did good to call me. It sort of fits in with my plans. Anything new, you call."

"Yeah. Later."

They hung up. The straight man went into his bedroom, and examined his guns. He chose the little .32.

He went to a supermarket, and got half a dozen boxes. He packed them. He paid his electric and phone bills. He packed a suitcase for himself. He placed the .32 in it. It was a Smith & Wesson revolver. A larger gun was too bulky, and heavier bullets tended to hit the target and keep on going. A .32 often has a tendency to keyhole when it hits something. If a .32 caliber bullet hit a man in the side it might come out his shoulder. The man never touched automatics. They could jam at a critical time.

A mini-storage outfit provided space for the boxes. The dealer from the cottage agreed to take over the payments on the compact. Another friend bought the Magnum. The straight man wrote his will. He visited various banks, converting some of his cash into Travelers Cheques. It took three days to make ready.

48/   The straight man sat in the bus, hour after boring hour, thinking about Jay and Ted. They were in for a surprise. The man sat in the back with a black alcoholic and sipped J.W. Dant until he fell asleep.

He awoke in the grubby, below sea level, legendary city of New Orleans. He hadn't been there since he'd been an artist. He'd never had any talent, he couldn't draw. He hadn't even been able to con the tourists.

When the straight man had lived in New Orleans, he'd had two roommates. They'd all shared a room on Bourbon Street. The rent had been eighteen a week. One of them, Norm, had made his money hustling pool. The other, Rich, had been a professional pan-handler. The man hadn't been good at anything. A tatooist had moved into the room next door, and set up shop. The man talked him into giving a split on every tatoo he hustled in off the street. After a week of hustling drunken sailors, he didn't want to see another tatoo. Rich finally got busted for soliciting funds while impersonating a priest, and Norm, after hustling the wrong people somewhere, had entered a hospital for an extended stay. The straight man had lost touch with them.

He stored his bag and walked the streets, hoping he'd bump into his ex-wife. She was supposed to be living with some old white hair. After a day he took a cab to the airport and bought a ticket for San Francisco. He had a responsibility there.

49/ It was supposed to be raining in San Francisco, and it was. It was a beautiful city. There were hills. It was green. It was cosmopolitan. It had neighborhoods. The straight man rented a room in the Tenderloin. He got a room with a bath and a mini-refrigerator for ninety dollars a month. The Tenderloin was the area where the whores, junkies, and old alcoholics lived. He gave an assumed name. There were no questions. He began his search.

The telephone book had no Xenos, but he found one in the nearby town of Sausalito. Carrying his piece, he took a bus, and watched the address for two days until he was positive it was wrong. The place appeared to be occupied by two or three gay men. They dressed well, and didn't seem to work, but they weren't Jay and Ted. The days drifted by. It was a great town for alcoholics. There were bars everywhere. He began to work his way through the neighborhoods.

He wasn't having any luck. Every morning he ate breakfast at a small Greek restaurant. The waitress liked him, and after a week she invited him to dinner. She didn't even know his name. He bought a bottle of Lancers, and went to her apartment. They ate rice, drank the wine, and went to bed. She was terrible in bed. The straight man began to eat breakfast elsewhere. He began to wonder if Jay and Ted were really in town.

50/ Ted stretched in his large double bed. He felt good. He rolled out onto the floor and began to do his daily sit-ups. He had eight thousand left from that rip-off down in Florida, a new wardrobe and a brand new .22 loaded with mini-mags. Jay was spending his money much faster, and would probably want to go to work again soon. Ted showered, shaved, and had a big breakfast. It was a beautiful day.

He walked down to Union Square and sat on a bench, watching the crazies, the hippies, the tourists, and the alcoholics. He lounged in the sun, breathing the good, clean air. He wandered over to where a crowd had formed, and watched a hilarious mime perform for donations. He felt so good, he gave a pan-handler a quarter. He walked into a health food store and drank a big glass of orange juice, digging the cute foxes walking by.

Ted began to get horny. He decided it wouldn't do any harm to take a long sauna, have a little massage, and maybe a little head. That chick Linda could sure give some head. He wondered if she would be working this early. He strolled toward his favorite massage parlor. The hostess told him he was in luck, Linda was working. She took his twenty dol-lars. He nodded, thanked her, and slowly undressed. He took a long sauna, there was no reason to hurry. He took a long, cleansing shower. He toweled himself off, lay face down on the massage table, and closed his eyes. Linda would be along soon.

51/ The straight man was frustrated. He'd wandered the streets of the city, drunk in dozens of bars, gotten phone numbers from various girls that didn't interest him much, and sat in various squares watching people. It was early afternoon and he needed to get laid. He decided to go to a massage parlor and see if they were really whorehouses.

He picked one at random. A cute hostess told him the rates. There were two sets of prices, but she didn't elaborate. The straight man took the most expensive of the least expensive set. He was shown into a room with a massage table and a chair. He disrobed and went into a small sauna room. A card on the wall said fifteen minutes was about maximum. He went to the shower next door. All the rooms, except the shower, had a small window in them. He lay down on the massage table and relaxed. An attractive brunette entered and began to massage him. After a while she asked if he wanted any additional massage. He didn't like the situation, and turned her down. She continued to massage him, and after washing him off told him the massage was over. He rose, and dressed.

As he was about to step into the hallway he saw Ted through the door window, leaving a shower. Ted entered another massage room. The straight man was right behind him. He hesitated, then looked in. It was Ted, lying down on the massage table, facing away from the door. The straight man looked up and down the hall. No one in sight. Forming his right hand into a karate *shuto,* he stepped quickly in, and next to Ted. There is only an inch or so difference between killing a man, and knocking him out. The man made no such mistake. In a moment he was back in the empty hall.

52/ The straight man sat on a stool in a bar that had a pool table. He ordered a draught beer and hunched over it, listening to the idle chatter. Several people had been gunned down for no apparent reason. Somebody was dressing as if she were fifteen years younger. The Giants had traded away their best young players again. The Arabs were unreasonable. Some guy had died in a massage parlor. The man asked a cab driver if massage parlors were really cat houses. The driver said he didn't know, and asked if the straight man was a cop. He told him he was on leave from the C.I.A.

The straight man bought a book. It was all about spies and exotic places and beautiful women. He took it with him as he carried his laundry up the hill to a small laundromat that was open twenty-four hours. He bought a box of soap and sat down with the book as his clothes were washed. Across the street was a row of apartment buildings. He glanced up from the book and froze as he watched Jay stroll out of a building. It was early afternoon, and Jay wasn't wearing a coat. The man looked away. Only predators stare, and everyone has some sort of built-in warning system.

Half an hour later the man gathered up his laundry and crossed the street to the entrance of the building Jay had left. There was the name: Xenos. Apartment four. The man carried his laundry to his apartment. He packed carefully, leaving out his traveling clothes. If he was lucky, he'd get him. He could always unpack. He cleaned the .32 and put it in his jacket pocket.

The plane ticket cost almost six hundred. The man paid cash. As he left the ticket counter he locked eyes with a beautiful Chinese girl. They smiled at each other. They spoke. They were going on the same flight. She was going to visit her grandparents on Taiwan. He asked if he could buy her a drink before they boarded. Flying made him nervous. She accepted with another smile. She had perfect teeth. He forgot his ex-wife, forever, again.

THE AUTHOR

KENT NELSON has spent time in Chicago,
Florida, Honduras, San Francisco, Las Vegas,
the United States Army and prison, not neces-
sarily in that order. *The Straight Man* is his first
work of fiction.